CRIMEN CONFLICT

CRIMEN CONFLICT
THE ORIGIN STORY OF MONSTERS™ BOOK SIX

MARTHA CARR
MICHAEL ANDERLE

DISRUPTIVE IMAGINATION

DON'T MISS OUR NEW RELEASES

Join the LMBPN email list to be notified of new releases and special promotions (which happen often) by following this link:

http://lmbpn.com/email/

This book is a work of fiction. All of the characters, organizations, and events portrayed in this novel are either products of the author's imagination or are used fictitiously. Sometimes both.

Copyright © 2023 LMBPN Publishing
Cover Art by Jake @ J Caleb Design
http://jcalebdesign.com / jcalebdesign@gmail.com
Cover copyright © LMBPN Publishing
A Michael Anderle Production

LMBPN Publishing supports the right to free expression and the value of copyright. The purpose of copyright is to encourage writers and artists to produce the creative works that enrich our culture.

The distribution of this book without permission is a theft of the author's intellectual property. If you would like permission to use material from the book (other than for review purposes), please contact support@lmbpn.com. Thank you for your support of the author's rights.

LMBPN Publishing
PMB 196, 2540 South Maryland Pkwy
Las Vegas, NV 89109

Version 1.00, June 2023
ebook ISBN: 979-8-88541-165-3
Print ISBN: 979-8-88878-438-9

THE CRIMEN CONFLICT TEAM

Thanks to our JIT Readers

Diane L. Smith
Dorothy Lloyd
Jackey Hankard-Brodie
Jan Hunnicutt

Editor

SkyFyre Editing Team

CHAPTER ONE

"Here we are, then."

The Volkswagen Golf crunched to a stop in the gravel parking lot. Halsey Ambrosius took in the wide two-story building that looked like it had seen better days. Including those when the roof had truly been thatched instead of built-up, painted, and covered in a light dusting of straw to make it look that way.

With a curiously reluctant smile, she turned toward the tall, dark-haired, bright-eyed young man sitting in the driver's seat and raised her eyebrows. "You drove all the way out to pick me up from the airport just to take me *here?*"

Seamus Havalon chuckled as he shifted into park and turned off the engine, his blue eyes sparkling in the afternoon sunlight. "Well, I did think it would've been a tad forward of me ta bring ye straight home after a flight like yers."

Despite the pressure slowly boiling beneath the surface of Halsey's relatively calm exterior since meeting Seamus at the Dublin airport, she laughed wryly. "You pretty much brought me straight home the last time I was here."

"Aye. But that's a bit of a longer drive than this." The young elemental from Ireland's Havalon Clan studied her face as he unbuckled his seatbelt, and the mischievous playfulness she'd seen on him more than any other expression faded into a concerned frown. "Besides, ye made it perfectly clear how badly ye need that pint. Who am I ta tell a lass she has ta wait?"

"Fair enough." After unbuckling her seatbelt, Halsey popped the passenger-side door of Seamus' car and looked through the windshield at the front of the pub outside the busiest metropolitan area of downtown Dublin. "And I honestly don't know how much longer I *can* wait."

She didn't miss the flicker of confusion passing across his brow before she pushed the car door fully open and stepped onto the gravel.

He didn't question her any further, though. Not right now, and not until they'd had the aforementioned pints. Halsey was grateful for that because she wasn't sure exactly how she might have answered any of his questions before she'd had a chance to sit down, gather her thoughts, and unwind with a good beer and a trusted friend.

Maybe more than a friend. If this was literally any other point in elemental history, maybe Seamus and I would already be something more. Damn it, if this were any other point in history, everything *would be different.*

The parking lot was decently full for early afternoon on a weekday, though Irish pubs and their patrons tended not to care too much about the time of day or the day of the week. Most of them didn't even care about the number of customers, sales, profits, or much else beyond maintaining the stability of a physical roof and an effective supply of booze. Through all her trips to Ireland, both before and after she and her cousin Brigham had discovered that damn silver coffin on the beaches of Moher, Halsey had learned what an Irish pub was.

It was community. Privacy. Safety.

Over the last few months, especially the last twenty-four hours, it seemed those three things had been vastly lacking in Halsey's life.

And here I am without Brigham. Again. About to spill my guts to a completely different elemental because I can't handle what's happening to me and can't face the look in my best friend's eyes when he finds out I've been carrying on one seriously messed-up Ambrosius family legacy. Secrets and lies. So let's walk into this pub, get everything off my chest with Seamus, then figure out a way to talk to Brigham about it all and actually do it this time, Hal. This has to stop.

As she crossed the parking lot toward the pub's front door, Halsey was so intent on berating herself into an open-hearted conversation with the gorgeous young Havalon elemental she'd only met a few months ago that she wasn't paying attention to much of anything else. The pub door stood in front of her. Seamus was somewhere behind her, his sneakers crunching across the gravel like her own. It was all that mattered.

Then something tingled across the back of her neck, making the hair there stand on end beneath her ponytail of thick, wavy dark hair she'd inherited from both her parents. It took her a moment to fully become aware of the sensation, which she probably wouldn't have paid any attention to if it had only lasted a few seconds before disappearing.

Yet the tingling sensation persisted long enough to drag Halsey from the depths of her internal monologue. That was all she needed to recognize it for what it was.

She'd felt it before, no less than eight hours ago.

The feeling of being watched.

It wasn't only the general sense of foreboding and instinctual hyperawareness she'd learned to hone through years of training and the last five years of hunting monsters. *That* was a feeling she'd quickly grown used to out of necessity. Recognizing when a monster may have caught her scent on the wind or noticed her presence before she and Brigham sprang into action to drive it back. Sometimes, the monsters *did* see her before she saw them, but only by a few seconds and only through the eyes of dumb, supernatural, instinct-driven beasts.

Beasts the Ambrosius Clan had been fighting since 953 AD when Cedric Ambrosius and his other elemental buddies discovered the wrecked Viking ship that had delivered the Blood Matriarch's newest wave of monstrosities to the shores of her enemies' home.

Halsey knew that feeling well. There were no beasts like that here today.

No, what she felt was the intense, intelligent, *sentient* stare of not only one or two pairs of disembodied eyes catching a curious glimpse of her from between the trees but of an entire *consciousness*.

She hadn't been able to pinpoint that feeling earlier this morning. Identifying the different sensations of being watched and cataloging each of their meanings hadn't been on the top of her to-do list in the middle of being ambushed—alone, without her partner, with no idea what she'd been up against.

That feeling was perfectly clear to her now as she crossed the relatively short distance between Seamus' car and the pub's old, warped, slightly crooked front door.

That *consciousness* was watching her. Studying her. Waiting for her to notice it and react in some way.

The same way the consciousness of the entire grindylow swarm had watched her this morning before rushing her in what had felt like a planned attack.

One she'd barely managed to escape through the most unusual means of survival so far, even for Halsey Ambrosius. And that was saying a lot.

The second she recognized that feeling, her body responded on its own without any cognizant command from her brain. She didn't notice herself slowing her purposeful march toward the pub because the only thing she could focus on now was the feeling of that collective intelligence burning into her and forcing her to pay attention.

That's impossible. I don't care what *those grindylows thought of me this morning. There's no way they could've made it out here as fast as I did. Even if the whole swarm zipped across the ocean from London to meet me here, they wouldn't be here* now. *They can't be...*

Trying to rationalize it all didn't change the feeling of an intelligent gaze lingering on her skin, boring into her mind, tickling along the top of her neck and the back of her head and down every extremity. It didn't change her suspicions about the source of the feeling, either.

The grindylows were here. Not just *any* grindylows but the ones that had almost torn her to shreds this morning before she'd used her copper orb for yet another last-ditch attempt to save her own skin.

It was impossible. Yet a better, more reasonable, more logical explanation wouldn't reveal itself.

She vigilantly scanned the front of the pub, the thin line of trees stretching behind the building and farther northwest into a thicker forest, and the relatively neatly pruned hedges and flowerbeds lining the crooked walkway in front. No ponds, no creeks, no water features, no grindylows. Still, the feeling of being intently watched wouldn't let up.

There's no way. Unless somebody bought the whole swarm a bunch of airline tickets and shipped them out on express delivery.

Under different circumstances, the thought would have made her laugh. After her long-awaited meeting with Halil Aydem this morning, however, not to mention the last-minute fight of her life that had ended in a grindylow swarm hastily obeying her every command, she wouldn't have found humor in anything right now.

Even if she'd had Brigham and his wry wit at her side.

A light breeze rolling across the beginning of the open Irish countryside punctured the stillness. The trees behind the pub rustled with fluttering leaves. The hedges and flowers bent beneath the wave of cool, late-summer air.

A flicker of bright, shimmering green blinked at her from behind the farthest pruned bush on the left.

Halsey froze, waiting for the shimmer to return, to move and reveal itself for what she already knew it was but couldn't admit to herself.

An eye. One wide, overly large eye glinted at her as it caught the sunlight. Then two, enormous and buggy in a squat, squashed face covered with knobby dark-green flesh like a horny toad. Three long fingers emerged from behind the same shrug, below those buggy eyes, to curl slowly around one of the lower-hanging branches.

Beseeching her.

Taunting her.

Confirming the impossible once again.

Shit. They're actually here. *Either that or every grindylow on the planet shares the same mind. Both options are completely fucking insane—*

"Hal?"

A warm hand settled gently on her shoulder, both startling her from her intense staring and reassuring her that she wasn't alone this time. Not like she'd been this morning under a literal grindylow ambush.

After sucking in a sharp breath, Halsey jerked her head toward Seamus and shot him a fleeting glance. "Yeah. I'm good."

"Aye?" The broad-shouldered young man who'd taken a liking to the Ambrosius Clan's best monster hunter from their first meeting towered over her by almost two feet. He had to dip his head to study her face. "Says quite a different ting when ye answer a question that hasn't even been asked yet."

"Sorry." Halsey couldn't help but return her attention to the far-left hedge where that grotesque little grindylow face had been staring back at her, but all signs of the creature were gone. Still, she had a hard time turning toward

Seamus because that would mean turning her back on what was in front of her, hiding and waiting.

For what? To attack her again or to swear some kind of impish fealty the way the others had this morning?

Finally, she managed to set all that aside to pretend she'd recovered. Right now, pretending was all she had left. "What were you going to ask?"

"Well, I aimed ta ask if ye were all right." Seamus dipped his head again to catch her attention, and this time, it worked. "Now I'm thinkin' that pint's more sorely needed than I t'ought."

"You have no idea..." The words tumbled from her mouth as she gazed into Seamus' bright-blue eyes. "So how about you float me the first round, and I tell you all about it?"

"Took the words right outta my mouth." The brilliant flash of Seamus' perfectly straight, startlingly white teeth when he grinned took her back to the day they'd met inside Faolán's Inn. Halsey had thought he was a member of the Havalon Clan Council at first. His size, his face hidden by a baseball cap, and his deep, booming voice could have belonged to anyone. That grin of his had convinced her she'd been wrong.

Seamus Havalon might have been the son of his elemental Clan's Council head, but he was unlike anyone Halsey had ever met.

She only hoped he could handle everything she was about to tell him over however many pints it took.

CHAPTER TWO

The pub's main front room wasn't particularly crowded, but Seamus still asked if any of their private side rooms were open when he ordered their first round. The bearded bartender in a collared shirt with tattoos covering both forearms nodded before pouring two large, cold, frothing pints of lager into frosted glasses. "Over'n the back right afore the jacks."

Halsey was worried she'd start drooling on herself when she picked up her glass, trying not to spill the thick head of foam over the sides. She fixed that problem by knocking down a good third of her first pint right there at the bar. It helped settle her nerves and made the men share an amused and impressed look.

"Leave us a tab open, eh?" Seamus slid a credit card across the bar as Halsey turned toward the private room the bartender had indicated. Then he leaned toward the other man and lowered his voice. "Any possibility of bringin' us another in 'bout t'erty minutes?"

The bartender's mustache twitched over the tiniest

smile as he raised an eyebrow. "Long as the place doesn't fill up faster'n she can knock 'em back."

"Much appreciated." With beer in hand, Seamus wasn't smiling as he turned away from the bar and headed toward the private room in the back, closest to the pub's restrooms. He put one on for Halsey as he walked through the frosted glass door, though she wouldn't have noticed a difference anyway.

She was already seated at one of two wobbly square tables, slumped back against the chair with one hand around her sweating pint glass on the table and her eyes closed.

"Now I *know* ye're not fallin' asleep on me." He laughed before the door swung shut behind him with a gentle click.

Halsey's eyes flew open, and she released a long sigh before offering him a small, tired smile. "Lager's not the same in the States as it is here. I've missed this."

"I hope a good pint isn't the *only* ting ye missed." His grin flashed again as he headed toward the open seat across the table from her. Her only response was another wry chuckle and one more long, smooth drink. Seamus set down his mug, effortlessly pulled out his chair to sit, and watched her with wide eyes until she was finished. "Maybe we should've started with *two* at the bar."

"That's just asking for trouble." She quickly wiped beer foam off her upper lip and onto her jeans under the table before shaking her head. "Honestly, knowing there's more where this came from is enough to keep me going. For now."

"Aye." Seamus lifted his glass toward her for a silent toast, which she quickly joined with her now half-empty pint. After he'd given himself a moment to appreciate the first sip of an ice-cold lager, he fixed his attention on the dark-haired, hazel-eyed young elemental across from him. His smile faded once more. This time, he looked like he was sitting down with a business partner or a fellow hunter rather than the cute girl he hadn't known long but had picked up at the airport for the chance to spend time with her.

Halsey supposed she was all three to him. Hopefully, that wouldn't change after they had what was sure to be one of the strangest conversations of both their lives.

"Ye may not've had yer fill of drink yet, Hal, but it's plain as day ye've run inta more'n enough trouble."

She forced herself to meet his gaze. "It's that obvious, huh?"

"Not that I'm a particular expert on all t'ings Halsey Ambrosius..." Seamus shrugged playfully and sat back in his chair. "Or not yet, anyhow."

"Cute."

Another self-satisfied smile flickered across his lips before he got back down to serious business. "I *do* know the look of a person who's been skippin' 'round the edge of losin' their mind. Gotta say, when I saw ye walkin' through the airport, I expected ye ta already be blathered right off the plane."

"Blathered?"

Seamus lifted his pint glass to demonstrate, emphasizing his point with a silent nod.

Halsey couldn't help a small laugh at the unexpected words still lost in translation between them despite the fact they were generally speaking the same language. "I don't drink on planes."

"Ah. The altitude, is it?"

"More like a safety precaution." She wrinkled her nose and took another quick drink. Even that simple explanation, while true, sounded thin and completely without substance, given her current situation.

"Ah, sure." Seamus nodded sagely. "Ye're dangerous enough as 'tis without the drink. Stands ta reason ye'd already know what the world's fixin' ta face when ye're a few pints in. *I* sure do."

Is he talking about the grand old time we had together at his family estate? Or the epic werewolf hunt afterward that ended with my axe in the silverback alpha's chest and one of his claws in my leg?

Either way, Seamus' insinuation didn't exactly have the intended effect. He was trying to lighten the mood by flirting and reminding her of the last time they'd seen each other face to face.

That had been months ago. Before Halsey had pieced together the mystery of her Clan Library's missing record and proof of the Mother of Monsters' release once before in the last thousand years. Before she'd unlocked so many more of the copper orb's abilities and discovered a few surprising new details about her own magic. Before she and Brigham had almost died multiple times and were forced to accept that the copper orb, Halsey's abilities, and all the changes to magic and monsters could no longer be ignored.

Focus, Hal. He's trying to break the ice. The least you could do is try *not to be a complete bummer.*

She decided to smile while she thought of an appropriate response, but it felt forced. "Well, what kinda message would it send if I walked right off the plane to meet you, reeking of booze?"

Seamus snorted. "Same message ye're sendin' now. Only I would've known ye'd taken a bit o' time to unwind from whatever's gotten ye so wound up ta begin with." He raised his glass again and slowly lifted it to his lips. "The fact ye haven't yet sends a whole different message in and of itself."

That made Halsey pause. Despite the tension still thrumming through her after one hell of a weird and concerning morning, her curiosity got the better of her. "What message is that?"

After his next sip of lager, Seamus looked on the verge of grimacing, though it had nothing to do with his drink. She knew it was serious when he held her gaze again and took a moment to judge his words before sharing them. "The kinda message that says ye haven't yet worked out *how* ye feel 'bout whatever it is. I like ta think I know ya well enough ta guess if ye haven't worked *that* out yet, it's bad enough and recent enough ta tear ye up like it is. O' course, I could be wrong…"

"You're not," Halsey blurted. It came out much more desperate than she'd intended, but almost everything about her current situation felt desperate. Now that she'd confirmed what he'd already guessed so easily, there was no point dancing around it any longer. "As recent as this morning, and as bad as… Well, I haven't been able to wrap my mind around it. If it's good. If it's bad. If it's totally insane and there's something really wrong with *me*—"

"Nah, don't start wi' that." Seamus shook his head, holding her gaze intently with another tiny, reassuring smile flickering across his full lips. "Ye aren't the kinda lass ta question what it is she's doin' or thinkin'. Not the Halsey *I* know."

She scoffed and grabbed her drink again. "No offense, Seamus, but I wouldn't say you and I know each other *that* well."

"Don't we?"

The look he gave her over his raised beer made her gut sink into a warm flutter of nervous excitement. Yet the intensity of everything else she'd been feeling for the last nine hours instantly gobbled up that sensation.

Before heading out to finally meet with Aydem, Halsey had been so sure she was doing the right thing. She would get the last crucial answers she'd been seeking about her magic and the golden orb, and she could go right home afterward and share it all with Brigham and their grandmother.

Of course, she also would have had to explain to her cousin that Aydem had contacted her right after they'd wrapped up their last mission in Coningsby, England. Most likely, he'd be furious with her for not telling him about it. Instead, she'd made a solo pit stop to meet the Order of Skrár member before she raced off to see Seamus Havalon.

Brigham would have gotten over it. They would have made amends and used the knowledge she'd gained to help the Ambrosius Clan and the other elemental families prepare for the final battle few of them wanted to believe was coming.

Instead, she'd received only cryptic answers from the man calling himself a purveyor of knowledge and claiming to know more about who Halsey was and what she could do than anyone else in her life. Including herself. She couldn't easily accept that, and she certainly couldn't take it back to Brigham without getting someone else's opinion on the whole affair.

Aydem might have specifically staged the grindylow ambush if someone from the Order of Skrár could even do such a thing. Or the whole might be one enormous and maddening coincidence. Either way, Halsey only knew one thing for certain.

An elemental monster hunter shouldn't be able to command an entire swarm of grindylows, or any type of monster, with their own natural magic.

Yet that was exactly what she'd done.

Halsey hadn't even noticed the silent, expectant pause in their conversation until Seamus chuckled wryly before clearing his throat.

"Don't get me wrong, Hal. There's always *more* we might know 'bout each other in the future. S'long as I don't screw the whole thing up by makin' ridiculous assumptions over our first pint—"

"Not ridiculous." She flicked her gaze to meet his and managed a smile. Seamus Havalon had given her exactly what she needed right now, and she could have laughed at herself for taking this long to see it.

They were friends. There was obvious chemistry between them and had been since they'd met, despite the fact she'd started out not wanting to take it any further than two young, slightly rebellious elementals helping each other and their prospective Clans as much as possible. They'd defended his home and his family together from the werewolves wreaking more havoc than they should have across the Irish countryside. It apparently didn't matter that Halsey and Brigham had unknowingly made the Havalons' werewolf problem worse when their mission last June had taken them to the Cliffs of Moher and that damned silver coffin. Especially when the Havalons had lauded Halsey for singlehandedly taking down the silverback alpha and living to talk about it.

Of *course* Seamus didn't know her like Brigham knew her. Nobody did. However, he knew her well enough to take her seriously. He liked her enough to genuinely want to help, and he was far enough removed from the Ambrosius Clan's secrets, lies, and family drama to make his opinion and any offered advice invaluable.

This little visit was exactly what she needed. She had to stop second-guessing herself long enough to accept whatever help, suggestions, support, and even a small amount of relief Seamus could offer.

So she did.

"Not that I'm an expert on Seamus Havalon," she started, playfully mirroring his words. "But for as long as we *have* known each other, none of your assumptions have been ridiculous. Or far from the truth, honestly."

He raised one dark eyebrow and leaned slightly forward, not quite daring to grin at the insinuation. "Not even one?"

Halsey couldn't help but laugh and decided it was best to hit the nail on the head so they could get past what was obviously taking up most of his attention right now. "If you're referring to how hard and fast you came on to me out of the gate the day we met, I'm not gonna sit here and tell you I didn't like it."

Seamus blinked in surprise, his head slightly jerking away from her like he couldn't believe she would actually say that out loud and to his face. Then he finally let one of those perfect, brilliant grins through the mask of his initial shock and laughed. "Ye really know how ta keep a lad on his toes."

"Well, when it's the only way to keep up with *me*, I kinda have to."

His booming laughter echoed around the small, private room. Hopefully, they wouldn't have any dire interruptions like the last time she was in Ireland.

At the same second, the frosted-glass door swung open. The bearded bartender strode in with a tray of not two but four fresh, ice-cold, frothing lagers balanced in one hand.

"Well shite, boyo." Seamus leaned back in his chair and failed at fixing the bartender with a confused frown. The fact that he was still laughing didn't help. "I did say every t'irty, didn't I?"

"Aye." The bartender nodded gruffly and set the beers down on the table one by one. "Figured that was a loose timeline. But one o' these rounds is straight from Ian McCraw. Saw the two o' ye walkin' in and wanted ta pass on a message. For the lad, good work. And for the lass…" The man set the last glass in front of Halsey and shot her a playful, unsmiling wink. "Good luck."

The friendly message from a stranger-to-her made her laugh.

Seamus clicked his tongue in mock irritation. "McCraw

always does know how ta make the damnedest impression. Tell him he can keep his nose outta the whole t'ing—"

"I'm a barkeep, not a postman," the man interrupted, his face expressionless despite the humorous tone. "Go tell him yerself."

He immediately took his leave after that, tucking the empty tray under one arm and walking briskly from the room. Halsey and Seamus were alone, both of them lost for words after such an odd message sent with a round of drinks from someone in the pub's common room.

"Well." Laughing, Seamus ran a hand through his hair, then stuck a thumb over his shoulder. "I can assure ye t'was an unexpected interruption."

"Either that, or you're a far better actor than I've given you credit for." They both laughed, then Halsey frowned at the frosted-glass door behind him as if she could see straight through to the room beyond. "Sounds like you know this Ian guy."

"Aye. Times like now, I wish I didn't." He drummed the fingers of one hand on the tabletop and tried to wave off the whole thing with the other. "Friend o' the family. The man's a nosey sonofabitch and a gossip ta boot. Not nearly as bad as his wife, but bad enough."

"Right." With a playful frown, Halsey warred between laughing the whole thing off and wondering if a harmless thing like a round of drinks from a gossipy family friend would come back to bite them in the ass. "You know, it kinda looked like you knew what he meant by 'good work and good luck.'"

"Aw, and *ye* couldn't suss out the meanin' of it on yer own?"

"You mean like I'm a catch, and you're more trouble than you're worth?"

It clearly took a lot of effort on Seamus' part not to burst out laughing again. For the first time, his nervousness looked a lot more genuine than his previous playfulness on their last meeting. He swallowed and cleared his throat again, but he was still smiling. "That about sums it up, aye."

"Well, Ian McCraw clearly has no idea who or what he's talking about."

"Ha. Clearly."

"But while we're here... What the hell, right?" Halsey grabbed her almost-finished first pint, knocked back the rest, then slammed it on the table with a contented sigh before picking up the next one. She lifted it toward Seamus over the table. Extra foam plopped onto the worn grain of the wood and ran down the sides of the glass and her fingers. "Let's give him something to gossip about."

Seamus' self-control broke down into another loud, booming laugh. He grabbed his drink to toast a man who couldn't mind his own business.

CHAPTER THREE

With her previously tense mood significantly softened and lightened, Halsey was happy to spend the next few minutes sipping away on free beer and cracking jokes with Seamus about this Ian McCraw guy. Apparently, the man had made Seamus Havalon's love life one among his quirky, frivolous dozens of hobbies over the last several years. Seamus was happy to allow it because it kept the old family friend from digging deeper into his family's personal lives.

Specifically, the fact that the Havalons of Ireland came from a long line of humans wielding elemental magic to fight off supernatural creatures and beasts without normal people ever knowing a thing about it.

Halsey wasn't sure if the Ambrosius Clan could have handled a "family friend" who looked so closely at any one of their personal lives without causing some serious damage. Her family was nothing like Seamus', though. When it came to decades-old secrets, webs of lies, and keeping everyone at a distance, including their own kin, she'd bet almost anything the Havalon Clan didn't even come close.

Seamus' family was united. Halsey's was broken, terrified, and scrambling to hold all the pieces together under fraying leadership. It didn't help that Halsey had drawn so much attention to the first chink in the Ambrosius Clan Council's armor, which had quickly grown into a spider web of cracks and holes that increasingly crumbled apart by the day.

More than anything, the differences between these two Clans, who had at one point been so supportive of each other, made it impossible for Halsey to truly enjoy herself. With the beer, the privacy, and the company she enjoyed as much as the last time, it would have been easy to brush aside all her worries and the burdens weighing her down. She didn't want to keep dealing with it all, day in and day out.

Who in their right mind would?

Halsey *was* in her right mind, though, despite how hard the Ambrosius Clan Council had tried to convince her otherwise before she'd stumbled upon the facts. Therefore, after a few minutes into their third round of drinks, she had to kill the playful mood by bringing up the much more urgent reason she'd come to Ireland this time.

At the next natural lull in the conversation, which unfortunately happened right after they'd finished laughing like crazy people, she finally decided she had to tell Seamus what was happening. For as little of it as she truly understood herself.

"Okay." She grabbed her glass for another long pull, which alerted him to the sudden change in mood. Then she set her drink down and looked him dead in the eyes. "Listen. Contrary to popular belief, I'm not a huge fan of ruining the mood."

"Ye sure 'bout that?" Seamus jokingly clicked his tongue. "*You?* One of t'most serious folks I've ever met? Can't be."

She had to force down a smile so she wouldn't get swept up in how good it felt *not* to be so serious. "This is great. You and me. Sitting here." Searching for the best next words, she gestured back and forth between them across the table. Fortunately, Seamus didn't prompt her for an explanation, most likely because she looked like someone trying hard to find the right phrasing. "And I'd love to keep doing this until they either run out of lager or kick us out…"

He snorted and gave her a short, oddly encouraging nod.

With a deep breath and a massive sigh, Halsey took the plunge. "But it's not the only reason I flew to Dublin to see you."

"Aye," he replied gently, his small smile unwavering. "I know it doesn't take nearly as many drinks ta warm up ta me, so I figured there was more to it."

"Like I said, none of your assumptions have been wrong so far." They shared another light, friendly laugh, but now it was tainted by the expectation that her "serious business" was about to become the sole focus. "But you're gonna have to bear with me, Seamus, okay? Because most, if not *all*, of what I can't believe I'm about to tell you is gonna sound insane. I do know that much."

"Even if it sounds insane, Hal, we both know it's only

the words and nae the person sayin' 'em." He spread his arms and dipped his head. "Would it make it a wee bit easier fer ya if I went ahead and started with a few guesses of my own?"

"Oh, you've already racked up an impressive list of *guesses*, huh?" Halsey took another long drink to steady herself, then released a bitter laugh. "All right. If your guesses come anywhere close to what this is, I'll... I don't know. I guess I'll have to—"

"Have dinner wit' me?"

She gaped at him and nearly choked despite already having effectively swallowed her last gulp of lager. "What?"

Seamus shrugged and smiled crookedly. "Not ta lessen the weight of what ye're carryin', o' course, but it felt like the right time ta bring it up."

"Oh." Blinking quickly, she tried to herd all her wayward thoughts about legitimate dates with Seamus Havalon into a closed corral in the corner of her mind so she could focus on the main reason she was here. "It definitely won't make this conversation any weirder than it's gonna be in a minute, so why not?"

"Aye?"

"Sure. Deal." She surprised herself by laughing like none of this was serious and they were simply two troublemakers having a little fun together. "If you can guess even...ten percent of what I've been through in the last three days, I'll let you take me out to dinner."

"Well, listen ta ye. Already not payin' attention, and we haven't even started yet." Seamus raised a finger to emphasize his next point, fighting to break into a grin. "I said ye'd have dinner *wit'* me. Not that I'd take ye out and pay fer the whole thing."

"I feel like those are the kinda details we can wait to hash out later."

"Aye, sure. Maybe ye're right..." He shrugged again, and the two young elementals managed to hold their composure for another three seconds before they started sniggering.

This is ridiculous, but I can't say it's not helping. And he knows it.

Pursing her lips through a coy smile, Halsey hid anything else she might have said behind a drink of beer, watching him over the rim of her glass the whole time.

Finally, Seamus clapped his hands and joined her in another drink. "Fine. I'll get ye warmed up, then."

"Hey, the beer's done a great job of that all on its own, but go ahead."

Their soft, hesitant laughter helped keep the mood light, but it didn't last long. Seamus dove right into trying to *guess* what Halsey had flown here from London to tell him instead of her own Clan. Not that Seamus Havalon was more likely to know what the hell was happening, but he was a lot less likely to ostracize her for it. Or turn her away and chalk it all up to the "crazy in her blood."

"Startin' wit' the most obvious first tends ta make for a smooth entrance," Seamus began, making them both laugh again. "Ye're here on yer own, obviously. Unless ye managed to stash yer wee cousin Brig-O inta one o' yer bags, which would make this even more impressive."

Halsey wanted to feed him a line or two to keep him going, but they'd made a deal, and she wouldn't tell him anything until he'd run out of guesses. She was positive he wouldn't come remotely close to the mind-bending truth of what the last forty-eight hours had brought into her life.

"No Brigh-O in the baggage, then." Seamus studied her expression before dipping his head in concession and continuing. "He knows ye're here, though. Can't leave somethin' like a visit ta Ireland outta the conversation wit' a person that important ta yer everyday. Nah, the two of ye're thick as thieves. And it ain't like ye have anythin' ta hide from him 'bout *me*, seein' as he was here wit' ye the last time. I'm sure he picked up a clue or two."

Halsey smiled and raised her glass to her lips again. "So you're starting with all the obvious details, huh?"

He laughed and sat back in his chair to fold his arms. "Oh, I'm just getting started. But I do have to ask for the sake of curiosity. Was he all that upset when you told him to go home without you while you stayed on this side o' the pond to visit me?"

"Maybe a little at first, but it didn't have anything to do with *you*. Mostly, he didn't want to sit across from Cavanaugh by himself and— Hold on." Frowning, she tilted her head and couldn't decide if she was still amused or thoroughly caught off guard. "I never said a thing about which side of the *pond* we were on. Or that Brigham was out here with me in the first place."

His flashing grin winked at her in the light as he spread his arms and said nothing.

CHAPTER FOUR

Halsey took another drink as she scrutinized her fellow monster hunter. The details he'd offered weren't the ones that concerned her the most. Yet they were eerily accurate. She hadn't so much as alluded to where she'd been or that she'd sent her cousin home so she could make not one more stop in the UK but two.

She set down her drink and turned her head slightly away from Seamus to eye him sideways. "So we're both on the same page here... If you've been stalking me and hacking into my phone or emails, things between you and me are gonna go in a very different direction."

"You mean you wouldn't be flattered?" Her snort of laughter was enough to keep him smiling before he added, "I wouldn't dream of encroaching on your privacy like that. Everybody needs a little. Adds a certain bit of fun to things, too, if you ask me."

"Sure, but right now, I'm asking you how you knew all that."

"Ah." He raised his pint glass toward her, then sighed as

he gestured over the table. "You only texted me back this morning to say you were on your way. The fact that you made it to Dublin by two o'clock tends to narrow down the list of places you could've flown in from."

Halsey blinked as she realized how little of a mystery this information would be to anyone paying attention, which she clearly hadn't been. At least not to the details of text responses and flight times. "Oh."

He shrugged off her surprise, though his broad smile remained. "Plus, I checked the flight schedules. Not that there weren't other possibilities, but hopping direct from Heathrow makes the most sense, given the timing."

"Of course it does." She tried to laugh with him as he revealed his not-so-sneaky sleuthing capabilities, but now it had become clear how much she was letting slip through the cracks of her own awareness with all the larger, more troubling problems she'd been facing. "Actually, it seems ridiculously obvious now."

"Aye, but that's only what's on the surface. I'm still working my way down." Seamus took another moment to consider what else he'd noticed about her since she'd made the last-minute decision to leave London behind as soon as possible.

His smile slowly faded as he studied her expression, and Halsey had the distinct feeling this guessing game of theirs was about to get a lot more serious. Maybe even so close to the truth that she wouldn't sound like a complete lunatic for bringing it up.

"You didn't come here just for a holiday on the Emerald Isle and a few pints with a handsome Havalon. You've got something to say. Something you need help sussing out from top to bottom. But we've been through almost three pints now, and for as little time as we've spent together, I *do* know you're not the kind o' person who dances around something important for fun. So you think I might be able to help, but you're not quite sure I'm the right person to tell." He raised an eyebrow. "How am I doing so far?"

For a moment, Halsey had no idea how to respond. *He's gonna nail this, and I'm gonna feel like an idiot for making such a big deal out of it. Might as well see how close he actually gets while I figure out how the hell I'm supposed to fill in the blanks afterward.*

She cleared her throat and dipped her head, trying to be casual. As if he hadn't started to unravel what she thought she'd been keeping locked up until now. "You're doing fine. Keep going."

"Ha. Fair enough." Seamus blinked into his pint, then regarded her with a sudden intensity that made her feel like she'd been stuck under a giant microscope. "I know how close ye are with yer cousin. Might've been the first thing I knew about you. O' course, I've got no problem admitting I know little to nothing about the finer points of coming up an Ambrosius instead of a Havalon, but I've heard a few things. From you and him last time ye both were here. From *my* Clan, however colorful those words might've been."

His reference to the longstanding feud between the Ambrosius and Havalon Clans, which Halsey and Brigham had known nothing about until they met Seamus, brought more levity to the situation. That made laughing about it together now a hell of a lot easier despite the heavy circumstances hanging over them.

Halsey's family had cared quite a lot more about the feud than any member of the Havalon Clan, as evidenced by the surprisingly warm welcome the Ambrosius cousins had received when Seamus had taken them to his family estate at the foot of the mountains. Even if things between their two families hadn't changed, more than a few views about any Ambrosius' willingness to play nice and work together had, including Halsey and Brigham's. More than anything, the community she'd felt with the Havalons had been enough to convince her that coming back for help with another kind of monster problem was the best solution at the moment.

"Hopefully, those colorful words are a bit rarer these days," she murmured, daring to flash another wry smile that didn't fully hide her trepidation.

"Oh, aye. Nothing but tall tales and praise for the Alpha Hunter in *our* halls."

Halsey clicked her tongue and lowered her gaze again, not sure she'd be able to maintain a relatively calm and composed exterior for much longer. Being referred to as the Alpha Hunter by one of the people who'd coined her new moniker didn't help much, either.

It wasn't a ruse. She *had* killed the silverback werewolf alpha. Alone, singlehandedly, and with one of her throwing axes to boot. But like she hadn't told Brigham about the alpha werewolf speaking to her with the voice of a man, begging her to deliver him a swift death and free him from his torment, she also hadn't clarified those crucial details to any Havalon. Including Seamus.

Whether he'd seen her visibly disturbed by the earned title or was merely dedicated to putting together the puzzle pieces on his own, Halsey had no idea. She couldn't stop staring at the worn, textured grain of the table between them that had probably been in this room since the pub first opened its doors. Knowing Ireland and its pubs, that might have been a hundred years ago. The only real way to know was to ask.

There's another big difference between us. Almost everything in his home has been around for centuries and will probably still be here for centuries after we're gone. Things don't change much out here. Not like the U.S. Not like Texas. My family's as old as his, but we're nowhere near as connected to the land we're trying to protect.

She had no idea how any of those thoughts were remotely connected to the conversation at hand. Even if she'd had the time to work it out, it was only another distraction to keep her from the real conversation she knew she had to face sooner or later.

It seemed Seamus had come to the same conclusion. He drew a deep breath, sighed heavily, and tapped a finger twice against the tabletop. "You're not here to talk about either of our families or whatever history still lies between them, though."

The low timber of concern in his voice finally made her look into his brilliant blue eyes again, and Halsey slowly shook her head. "Not quite."

"Aye. You came alone, last-minute, looking like you just clawed your way out from beneath the rubble of something…"

"Wow, really?" With a wry laugh, she spread her arms and looked down at her plain gray t-shirt beneath her dark-green canvas jacket. "Didn't think I was *that* much of a mess."

"Well, that was a metaphor." Seamus' brief flicker of a smile heralded a new understanding that he was about to hit home with his deductive reasoning. "The trouble ye're facing isn't. You and Brigham went your separate ways from London. If he'd known anything was bothering you, as this clearly is, he wouldn't have let you come out here on your own. Not that kinda bloke. On the other hand, if he *did* know and still felt comfortable enough leaving you on your own for a quick hop to Dublin, the thought of sharin' it with me wouldn't be makin' ye so fidgety. Which means he doesn't know what's happened."

Her hand moved to snatch her pint glass again. The next thing she knew, she was guzzling the last of her drink while her friend fell deeper down the rabbit hole and toward the truth.

"Maybe ye hadn't been planning to come see me at all, if ye had other things in mind. Maybe ye did. Doesn't really matter because the best way to send the lad home was to tell him you were comin' out here anyway. Honestly, I don't mind being used as an excuse. Only means he knows ye feel somethin' about *me*, and I'll take it as a compliment either way. Obviously, though, there's much more to it.

"If I had to guess, I'd say whatever it is that has you all shaken up happened after good ol' Brig-O decided it was safe enough and harmless enough to leave ye on yer own. But ye didn't tell *him* about it even in a phone call. Which tends to be a choice people make when revealing the whole truth also means they'd have to reveal parts they'd been keeping secret for a lot longer than they should've."

Finally, Seamus' constant string of voiced thoughts from one conclusion to the next paused. At the same second, Halsey drained the last of her third pint and practically slammed the empty glass on the table with a bang.

When she looked up at him with wide eyes, she found him already staring at her. A slight frown creased his dark eyebrows.

His blue eyes flickered from her face to the empty glass and back. "Clearly, Hal, you're bursting at the seams to tell *someone*. I'm glad it's me. And for what it's worth, there's no reason on my end for you to feel guilty 'bout comin' to me with whatever this is before having a gab about it with yer cousin. If it's a secret you need keepin', I hope you know you can trust me."

After taking a long, deep breath, Halsey held it and pressed her lips together. Her throat and chest burned with the large quantity of lager and carbonation she'd slammed down. The only response she could manage was a quick nod.

"Well, that's a relief." Seamus chuckled softly, and when she still wouldn't look at him, he leaned forward and folded his hands on the table. His gentle, caring gaze with a fervent curiosity that rivaled her own, combined with most of a slammed pint, brought a hot flush into her cheeks. But he still wasn't finished. "So let's get down to the meat of it, Hal. What kinda trouble did ye get yerself into that's so bad you have to keep it from *him* and came to tell *me* instead?"

The breath she'd been holding burst out of her, which only added to the growing lightheadedness brought on by the conversation and three pints. Seamus had successfully unraveled half of her massive dilemma without knowing any of the details. Huffing a laugh that sounded more like a choked gasp, she opened her mouth to reply with something she hoped would sound reasonable and sane. Something that might help this conversation glide smoothly from this first guessing phase and into the next.

Instead, she blurted, "Christ, you're good at that."

Concern and a surprising twinge of embarrassment tinged his gentle chuckle. "Aye, well… It's a gift *and* a curse. Don't get me wrong. I'm entirely interested in what ye have to say. However, there's one thing I want to make clear and settle right now before ye dive in."

Great. I totally freaked him out without having to say a thing, and now we need ground rules. I'd probably do the same thing if I were him. And he'll probably never wanna see me again after this.

She steeled herself for the inevitable hardline boundary any sane person would erect to protect themselves when faced with a looming confession like this, then swallowed and nodded curtly. "Sure."

With pursed lips and a contemplative frown, Seamus returned the nod as if grateful to hear she was open to it. His slightly alarming seriousness made his next words pack more punch. "I think we can both agree I came damn near close enough to the truth. So, after ye've gotten this off yer chest, ye're out of excuses to keep me from taking you out to dinner."

Halsey balked. "To…dinner?"

"Food. Drinks. The two of us. So there's no confusion, it *will* be a date. Ye already agreed."

It was the last thing she'd expected him to say, but he was right. They'd made that deal before she'd had any idea

Seamus Havalon was as good at piecing together mysteries as he was at rebelling against his Clan Council's wishes to ignore two rogue Ambrosius elementals who'd reached out for help.

After quickly collecting herself, she grinned. It actually felt genuine, considering how much pressure she'd been carrying around with her. "Well, you sure as hell earned it."

CHAPTER FIVE

Now that Seamus had broken the ice with his uncanny guessing ability, Halsey found it easier than she'd expected to deliver on the details. Once she started, the floodgates of everything she'd been keeping to herself for what felt like an eternity opened wide to let it all come spilling out. After that, nothing short of being physically attacked could have stopped her until she was finished.

There were plenty of things she hadn't told anyone, including her grandmother, who still knew more than anyone else. Yet Halsey's need to get the most recent weight off her chest made it impossible to start at the beginning. Instead, she recounted recent events out of chronological order, starting with the surprising email she'd received from Aydem after finishing her last mission with Brigham in Coningsby.

She described how many times she'd tried to meet with Aydem before then, and how each scheduled meeting was subsequently canceled without any real reason beyond the fact that Brigham had been physically with her each time.

When she mentioned wanting to meet with a representative from the Order of Skrár, Halsey didn't feel the need to tactfully leave out any mention of the copper orb she'd transmuted from the leftover sand in her family's acquisitions warehouse in Dublin. Not like she had during her recent debriefings with Brigham and Cavanaugh after a string of missions the Ambrosius cousins wouldn't have survived—let alone successfully completed—without the orb.

Meeting with Halil Aydem to get some answers about the orb and its magic, as Greta had intended with her cryptic suggestion of "asking the living records," had finally seemed like a possibility. She had no problem telling Seamus what she hadn't told Brigham about Aydem's email asking her if she could get away from her busy schedule to meet him in London. The man had clearly only wanted one Ambrosius elemental to be present for their conversation, and that one had to be Halsey.

Of course, she and Aydem had different ideas of what that meeting would entail. She'd walked onto that private property thinking she was safe. That someone from a secret Order dedicated to preserving the historical records of the magical world would be willing to alleviate the confusion of one young elemental monster hunter. She'd truly thought he meant to help her make sense of the changing world now that the Mother of Monsters had returned. On top of that, she'd trusted that someone claiming to exist in service to "the living records" could tell her what the copper sphere was and why it was affecting her magic the way it had.

She'd been so incredibly wrong.

Describing the way Aydem had goaded her into anger and frustration with his circular conversation, answering nearly all her questions with questions of his own that hinted at her lack of knowledge about *herself* was easy. The hard part was pushing through to what came next after Aydem had told her to use the orb however she saw fit and to pay attention to the ways it obeyed her. He'd said *that* would give her the only answer she would ever need to understand how she fit into the "grand scheme."

That the orb's magic connecting with her own was her *birthright*.

None of those things had made sense at the time, and they still didn't make sense as Halsey described the incredibly odd encounter.

The time came to continue her story with the overwhelming numbers of grindylows that had ambushed her in the park, surrounding her with hundreds of buggy eyes while Aydem laughed and disappeared into the remaining shadows. Halsey choked on the words and almost didn't think she could keep going.

Fortunately, the bearded bartender's impeccable timing saved her as he walked in with two freshly poured pints. Knowing how to read the room, he set the drinks on the table without a word, collected the empty glasses while making zero eye contact, and quickly left his patrons to their privacy.

Halsey downed almost half her pint in one breath before she felt like she could continue.

"If I'd been anyone else..." She absently swiped at the beads of condensation dripping down the glass. "There's no point trying to sugarcoat it. If I'd been anyone else, I'd be dead. I've never seen a swarm of grindylows that big. Elemental magic didn't do anything. They would've ripped me apart limb from limb. Probably would've hidden all the evidence in seconds, and no one would have ever known what happened."

After swallowing thickly, she inhaled and pushed herself to continue. "You know, I don't think it would've been any different if Brigham had been there with me for backup. These things were… Shit. They were worse than the chimera."

"There's a chimera now, too?" Seamus asked softly, interrupting her storytelling for the first time.

With *that* as the first question he'd asked throughout her entire tale, Halsey nearly laughed. "Oh, yeah. I should probably touch on that eventually. Guess that's what I get for not technically starting at the beginning."

"No, I let myself get distracted. That's on me." He slowly shook his head, studying her face with an open curiosity that hid whatever other thoughts were jumbling his mind right now. "You're doing fine, Hal. Keep goin'."

"Yeah." She almost took another massive glug of beer, then figured it was better to push herself through with her willpower still intact instead of drowned by too much booze to the brain. So she left the pint glass on the table, keeping her hand wrapped lightly around it just in case. Then it was a lot easier to look into Seamus' eyes and finish the story she'd been terrified to recount out loud.

Because speaking it made it undeniably true.

Now I kinda get why it was so much easier for my family to keep their own secrets locked up so tightly for so long. Talking about this shit is almost as bad as the real thing.

Still, she pushed herself to continue through the fear and confusion. If anyone on the planet was sufficiently prepared to hear her strange confession, it was Seamus Havalon. Even if he wasn't the most qualified person to hear it, he was what she had right now. She'd already come this far. *Not* finishing would probably make her explode. And exploding in a Dublin pub wasn't nearly as safe and predictable as exploding on Greta Ambrosius' front lawn on their family's private property along a Texas greenbelt.

"Seamus, I..." She drew another sharp breath, then cleared her throat. "I know this sounds insane, but I really thought I was done. I thought I would die right there in the park. That I'd fucked up so badly, and no one would ever know. That *Brigham* would never—"

The memory of it, still so fresh from early this morning, made her choke on her words again. Seamus didn't move a muscle or say a thing, knowing she didn't need any more prompting but would get to it when she was ready.

Halsey didn't know if she'd ever truly be ready, but it was now or never.

"I wasn't thinking when I used the copper orb again. It was just...in my hand, and all I could think was that I didn't want to die. It couldn't end that way, because there's still so much left to... I couldn't..."

"There's nothing wrong with feeling any of that," Seamus replied gently. "Trust me. Even the best monster hunter around is allowed to feel like they want to live to see another day. You have to know there's no shame in it."

"No, I do. I know. Of course. But that's not the part that feels so much harder to say than I thought it would." Halsey closed her eyes and inhaled deeply to steady herself.

She couldn't open her eyes again when she added, "I got myself into a bad situation. Made a pretty epic mistake there. You can tell me even the best of us make mistakes too, Seamus, but the best of us *don't* end up using magic they don't know how to explain."

"Sounds like ye *did*, though."

She opened her eyes and found the same open, compassionate, supportive gaze waiting for her from across the table. Maybe even waiting to catch her if she needed it. She sure as hell felt like she was on the verge of falling.

"This orb I made at the warehouse, the thing I *created* from someone else's leftover magic because I wanted to make it easier to carry home with me…" A bitter laugh escaped her. "It's always responded to me. How I feel. What I want. What I *need* when I'm too blindsided by what's in front of me to figure it out. It responded to me at the park this morning, which isn't all that strange based on personal experience. The problem is *how* it responded."

"Can't have been all that bad." He attempted another smile to lighten the load of her story. Though she wasn't able to smile back, seeing it from him helped. So did his encouraging nod when he added, "You're alive. You're here in one piece. If you ask me, I'd say only that matters."

Part of her wanted to break down sobbing. Part of her wanted to leap to her feet, and overturn the table, fresh pints and all, then run as fast and as far away from Seamus Havalon's empathetic gaze as she possibly could before inevitably collapsing. Surprisingly, yet another part of her wanted to climb *over* the table, grab his face in her hands, and kiss him like it was her last day on Earth and her last chance to kiss anyone.

Halsey mentally stomped on all those urges. She tucked them into a tiny corner of her mind and forced herself to do the one thing she *didn't* want to do. "Even if the orb has affected my magic so much that I didn't *have* to keep fighting?"

His wide eyes narrowed for a split second before he tilted his head in confusion. "As in ye discovered something new in ye and blasted 'em all to kingdom come at once?"

She shook her head. "As in, I discovered something new in me that made the grindylows stop. That made them...*obey*."

The ensuing frown creasing Seamus' features was what she'd expected and dreaded seeing. Because of course he still didn't understand what she was saying. "Obey what, Hal?"

She swallowed and stiffly muttered, "Me."

Then she snatched her half-empty pint and downed the rest of it because the story was out, and she couldn't look at him any longer. She couldn't bear to see the confusion, disbelief, and, worst of all, the fear she knew would linger behind his eyes. Seamus could pinpoint the crux of her current dilemma by playing Sherlock Holmes over a few drinks, and he could act as carefree and playful as he wanted with another normal elemental who might have been good for him once upon a time.

Yet what Halsey had confessed wasn't normal. Even a monster hunter with the best poker face couldn't possibly hide the awful reaction she knew her statement had evoked.

Halsey Ambrosius had controlled monsters with her own magic, and that was certainly something to fear.

She sure as hell feared it. Why wouldn't anyone else?

Chugging down the second half of her fourth pint didn't make her feel any better, but it had given her something to do. A few brief seconds were all she needed to steel herself against what she knew she'd find in Seamus' gaze. Now that she'd said it all out loud, it was true, and she could live with that. She'd have to live with others' opinions of her too. Even that seemed so much easier.

When she finally forced herself to look at him again, Seamus had already slumped back into his chair with his arms folded. As he frowned at the table, one hand rose to slowly rub back and forth beneath his bottom lip.

Of course he's gonna take a minute. Who wouldn't need time to process this? Then he'll realize I'm not joking, he'll tell me to get the hell out of Ireland, and we can both kiss that dinner date goodbye.

It took him so long to respond that she couldn't keep waiting. "Well?"

He raised his eyebrows but kept staring at the grain of the old polished wood table and said nothing.

"Seamus." Halsey bit her lip, searching his face for any sign of what to expect so she could prepare herself for it. "Please say something."

"Aye." His frown deepened as he cleared his throat. "Well, I *can* say that certainly wasn't like anythin' I'd expected ta hear."

"I feel like that goes without saying." Her attempt to laugh it off fell flat, but not getting anything else from him was even worse. "Listen, I know this whole thing sounds crazy. And I totally get it if you think I'm insane after this, but I—"

"Ye do?" Seamus finally looked at her. "'Cause I sure as shite wouldn't understand it meself."

"Yeah, it's a lot to wrap your head around—"

"If I'd sat here for as long as I have, listening to every word you said and watching you put yerself through that kinda hell all over again, only ta think ye'd gone and lost the plot entirely, there'd be a lot more wrong with me than there is with you."

His words caught her off guard. She opened her mouth to reply, but nothing came out. The click of her jaws clamping shut again after feeling like a gaping fish seemed to clear her mind. "Well, now I feel like we're talking about two different things," she told him.

"Yer feelings are right on track. Was that a hell of a tall tale ye shared? You're damn right it is. But I'm not talkin' 'bout yer story, Hal." A tiny smile flickered at the corner of his mouth, which surprised her more than any of his other reactions. "*That* I believe, well and truly. What I *can't* seem to quite get past is that all this time, you've been expecting me ta turn ye away just for tellin' it."

She blinked furiously, sucked in a sharp breath, and tried to pull herself back together. "So you...*don't* think I'm crazy?"

He picked up his pint for a small, thoughtful sip, then shook his head. "Ye're no madder than the rest of us, trust me. A man who turns away someone he cares about because he doesn't like what he sees when they take down their walls? *That's* what makes a person crazy. I know that's not where *you* are, Hal, and I don't intend to go down that road meself anytime soon."

It was tempting to let herself get caught up in his roundabout way of saying he cared for her. That would have been an easier topic to focus on right now. But Halsey had become a master at focusing on the things that confused her the most. The missing puzzle pieces she needed to create a cohesive whole she could study and actually understand. Her insatiable curiosity only added to that particular skill set, which meant she had to clarify the most important part of this first. Then maybe they'd get to the part about defining their relationship in more concrete terms.

So she sat back in her chair, waited until she wasn't stunned anymore, and raised a dubious eyebrow. "I want to make this perfectly clear. You're saying you believe everything I told you? Like, you're just taking me at my word?"

"Bloody hell, Halsey." Seamus barked a laugh of disbelief. "Your word's never been in question."

"Well, not in *this* country, apparently," she quipped, tossing her arms in exasperation. The words had spilled out without her knowing what she was saying, backed by all the pent-up tension, uncertainty, and bewilderment that had been churning inside her since she peeled herself off the grass in that park and realized she was still alive.

As soon as she'd said it, though, she clamped her mouth shut again and stared in shock at Seamus. He'd taken the whole thing in stride, far better than she'd dreamed possible.

Seamus also looked surprised. However, his wide-eyed shock disappeared beneath an unintended snort. Seconds later, they both laughed wildly together as if the whole thing had been one enormous joke.

What made it even funnier was the fact that her offhanded, irritated comment was true. If she'd gone to her own family about this new discovery, she had no doubt the Ambrosius Clan Council would have turned her away as swiftly and mercilessly as the day she'd called an emergency meeting to tell them about the silver coffin. Seamus hadn't, though. The rest of the Havalon Clan wouldn't turn her away, either.

Right now, despite having no idea what her newfound powers meant or why she'd been singled out to wield them, Halsey was exactly where she was supposed to be.

CHAPTER SIX

"Do you have it with you?" Seamus held open the front door of the pub with one hand and gestured toward the gravel parking lot with the other.

"Have what with me?" Halsey slipped past him, her boots crunching the bits of gravel that had kicked up onto the front walkway during the day. "You already paid for all our drinks, and thanks for that, by the way. What more could a guy want?"

He snorted, followed her outside, and let the pub's front door swing shut with a groan of its hinges. "Ah, you know. Just a peek at the ol' copper ball that makes ye grow new magic overnight. Simple request, really."

"Oh, sure." With a smirk, she reached into her jacket pocket for the cold, smoothly rounded surface of the magical object in question. Then she pulled it out and swung it in front of his face. "You mean *this* one?"

"Shite, Hal." He quickly wrapped an arm around her shoulders, pulled her closer, and hunched over to hide the orb with his other hand. He looked around the parking lot to make sure no one could see. "Ye don't think maybe this is something that *shouldn't* be aired in public where any regular folks can see?"

"Wow, you're starting to sound like Brigham."

Seamus straightened to look at her with mild distaste. "Well, now you're just makin' this weird."

"Says the guy freaking out for no reason." Halsey grabbed the hand he was using to shield the orb from view and gently pried it away. "And yes, there's no reason to worry about this thing. Not when it comes to normies, anyway."

He didn't look convinced. "What a cute thing to call 'em."

"Pretty sure one of my older cousins started that. They can't see it."

"Your cousins?"

"The *normal folks*, Seamus." His continuous confusion made her laugh again as they reached his Volkswagen. She broke away from him to head for the passenger-side door. "Trust me. I've been about as blatant with this thing as I could possibly get in front of regular humans. The last time I used it with an audience, it was in front of almost an entire village. Nobody saw the orb, and nobody saw its magic."

He stopped beside the driver-side door, towering over the roof of his car and eyeing the orb in her hand. "Or yours, yeah?"

"Come on. You know they can see elemental magic. Hence all the *secret monster-hunter* business, right?"

"Aye, but that's not the kind I meant."

"Yeah, I know…" She wrinkled her nose at the orb in

her hands. Fortunately, the thing had remained silent, cold, and inactive throughout their conversation in the pub. She hoped it would continue to do so for the duration of her stay in Ireland, even if that only happened to be a few days.

Wouldn't it be nice not to get interrupted by another emergency? A girl can dream, I guess.

"Here." She tossed the orb over the roof of the car, and Seamus grunted as he fumbled to catch the thing and not make a scene in a public parking lot where any normie could see.

"Shite." He looked like he wanted to toss the thing right back at her, but then he paused to study it closer, turning the thing over and over in his hands. After a few seconds, he looked around the parking lot again with a confused frown. "Ye're certain no regular folks can see this thing?"

"Trust me. That might be the *only* thing I know for sure about the fun little puzzle you're holding."

"All right. I'll take your word for it." Still frowning, he raised the orb so she could see it over the top of his car and added, "I don't suppose you'll be telling me next that it turns a person invisible, too, eh?"

Halsey snorted and opened the car door. "Nope. If anyone were even out here watching, they wouldn't see that thing. They'd definitely see you holding up your hand like you're waiting to catch something, though."

"Waiting to…" Seamus looked at the orb raised in his hand, then realized how ridiculous he must have looked to anyone who couldn't see he was holding something. Clicking his tongue, he opened the door and slid behind the wheel next to a laughing Halsey already in her seat. "Very clever."

"It's like you said." She elbowed him playfully in the side. "If I'm no madder than the rest of us, it only makes sense that we all look a little nuts from time to time."

"Ha. Speak for yerself." Chuckling, he handed over the orb and waited for her to take it from him before sticking his keys in the ignition and starting the car.

Halsey smirked and pocketed the sphere again before strapping on her seatbelt.

Okay. That wasn't nearly as bad as I expected. Any of it. Definitely didn't think he'd be asking about the orb right up front, but it's a good sign, right? He's not freaked out. He's not pretending to believe me. Maybe I actually made the right choice coming here.

After the heavy burden of her newest magical discovery, the idea that she could be sitting comfortably in Seamus' car, talking and laughing and tossing the damn copper orb around like she didn't have a care in the world, felt almost too good to be true. Which meant Halsey intended to soak up every moment of it because, in her experience, the incredibly good things tended not to last as long as the chaos.

Only after Seamus had pulled out of the gravel parking lot and headed away from the city toward the open Irish countryside did he continue the conversation. It didn't surprise her that he still wanted to question her more about the bauble, but thankfully he'd picked a topic she felt comfortable discussing. With him, anyway.

"So you transmuted a bunch of sand into copper," he started, glancing briefly away from the stretch of road in front of them to check her lap. His nose rumpled when he realized she'd already put the orb away, but it seemed more in amusement at his own curiosity than disappointment. "That in and of itself is something else."

"Changing the elemental composition of *any* natural resource?" Halsey laughed. "Tell me something I don't know."

"Well, I was hoping you'd be the one to tell *me* a thing or two."

She shot him a quick sidelong look and found him grinning at her before he returned his attention to the road. "Okay, go ahead. What do you wanna know?"

"That's a rather long list at the moment. Most of which I suppose can be checked off by asking, 'What else can that thing do?'"

Halsey settled her head against the headrest and watched the late-summer green of the rolling Irish hills passing them by. She drew a deep breath. "Way more than I thought possible when I made the stupid thing. That's for sure."

"Goes without question." He leaned slightly toward her and murmured, "But that's not an answer."

"Oh, you mean you want *specifics*. You do ask an awful lot of a girl, Mr. Havalon."

Seamus straightened in his seat and grabbed the steering wheel with both hands before letting out a low whistle. He couldn't help but grin at her again, his attention split between wanting to watch Halsey and needing to watch the road. "Well, ye're not makin' it any easier, Miss Ambrosius."

That made her bark out a laugh. The exchange somehow seemed to cement the knowledge that she could tell him literally anything and not have to worry about how it might be received, misconstrued, or used against her.

She told him everything, from beginning to end. The day she'd discovered in Greta's living room that the copper orb responded instantly, not only to her emotions but to her intentions. Even before they formed in her mind. The strange glow and hum coming from the thing that had kept her up a few nights in a row with no reasonable explanation. The fact that the copper orb had been literally the only way to kill an unkillable chimera, and only by letting the artifact's magic tear the beast apart into three separate and whole pieces of itself.

Finally, there was the surprising realization in Coningsby that the orb's magic had somehow fused with her own in order to heal Brigham from a barghest wound that would have left him permanently incapacitated but infinitely unable to die. Recounting the insane idea she'd had to heal all the barghest victims in the village—by making them drink a fake healing potion spiked with grains of the orb's magic—was the cherry on top.

By the time she finished that last story, Halsey hadn't expected Seamus to burst out laughing the way he did.

She smiled crookedly and shifted in her seat so she could better scan him. "Hey, it's good to know you think over a hundred wounded civilians exposed to magical poison, monsters, and *elementals* up close and personal is so hilarious."

Seamus shook his head and kept laughing for a moment before he managed to pull it together. "Surely you don't think so little of me as to believe that."

"Well, then, why are you laughing?" Despite her

attempts to sound serious about it, Halsey's own amusement echoed in her voice.

When he shot her another quick look, a sheen of tears glimmered in his eyes. "The way you tell these stories, Hal. It's like listening to my granddad complain about all his sons."

"*What?*" Now she was laughing with him, and she still had no idea why. "What does that even mean?"

"It means ye've a gift for storytelling. That's what. No matter how bloody awful it was while you were in the thick of it."

"Eh, the super-powered magical healing wasn't all that bad." Halsey shrugged and looked back out her window at the green grass and the blue sky stretching out around them. "Freaked Brigham out, though."

"Ye don't say."

"Freaked me out, too, honestly. Being able to *feel* it all, like I'd been cut up into hundreds of tiny pieces…" The car fell silent before she shifted again and cleared her throat. "Sorry. That was a weird thing to say. I don't know why I even brought it up."

"Ye brought it up because it needed ta be said. That kinda thing always finds a way out, one way or another." After sniffing and blinking back the tears of laughter threatening to spill out, Seamus looked quickly back and forth between her profile and the road. "Ye don't have ta apologize ta me for anythin' ya feel like sayin', Hal. I do mean that."

"Well, thanks."

"Aye, and maybe one of these days, you'll actually believe it."

They both laughed, then Halsey found one of her own questions begging to be asked. "So now that you've heard all there is to know about the magical Twilight Zone I've been living in for the last few months…"

He sniggered and checked the rearview mirror. "Aye?"

To finish her thought, Halsey had to look directly out the front windshield. Even in her own mind, the question sounded ridiculous. "Any chance you might know what the hell's happening to me?"

"Ah…" Seamus scratched an eyebrow with a thumbnail and looked both at a loss and confused by his lack of knowledge. "Wish I did. Then I could use it as leverage for a second date."

"Ha! Before we've even had the first one?" She shook her head with a playful sigh. "Somebody might be getting ahead of himself a little."

"Nah. I don't need to finish the first date to know that one won't be nearly enough." Then he shrugged and tilted his head toward her. "Though it sounds like ye're the one with uncertainty in that department, so it's probably best I don't have any overly valuable advice ta give ya."

"Okay, listen." Halsey thrust a finger in the air to correct him. "If there was any potential *uncertainty* on my end, I wouldn't have made that deal with you in the first place."

"I see…"

When he didn't say anything else, she turned toward him and leaned forward to catch his attention.

Once more, Seamus graced her with that brilliant grin of his. "And there it is."

"What?"

"That right there's the closest you've come to actually sayin' ye're at least a little fond of me."

She grinned, leaned back, and returned to staring out the windshield. Whether it was the weight of having finally unloaded her secrets to someone she could trust, the buzz of four pints in half as many hours, or the fact that Seamus' text had come at the perfect time, Halsey didn't mind the flirting one bit. For the first time in a long time, she felt comfortable enough not to pretend she did.

"All right, you got me," she admitted with a shrug. "I might be a *little* fond of you."

"That's excellent." Seamus tried to stifle another grin. "And the feelin' might be mutual."

"For now."

"Understood."

"So don't let it go to your head."

He laughed and managed to smother it beneath an obviously fake frown. "No, certainly not. We can't have any o' *that*, now, can we?"

She huffed a laugh and shook her head.

Well, look at you, Hal. This morning, you thought you were gonna die. And now you're sitting in a Volkswagen Golf with Seamus Havalon, saying ridiculous things and thinking about your date with him instead of your job. I mean, at least I'm not actually on *a job.*

Riding in silence beside the handsome young elemental wasn't by any means an unpleasant experience. But as usual, Halsey couldn't keep her growing curiosity at bay. She propped her elbow on the armrest, held the side of her head, and turned to look at him again. "So where *are* you taking me for this date number one?"

"Hmm. Ya know, with all the excitement at the pub, I hadn't had the chance to settle on a place. Not to worry, though. I'll have it figured out by tomorrow."

"What? *Tomorrow?*"

"Aye." He shot her a playful frown. "Unless, o' course, ye already had plans with someone else and didn't think to mention it."

"No, I don't have plans with someone else..." Halsey scoffed and tried to shake off her confusion with humor. "I wouldn't insult either of us like that."

"Also good ta know."

"Great. Well, if we're not going out to dinner together, where the hell are we going?"

His lips quirked again in a poor attempt to keep a straight face. "Now, I didn't say we *weren't* goin' ta dinner..."

"Seamus."

His composure broke, and he finally grinned before returning his attention to the road. "Hal."

"Where are you taking me?"

"All good things to those who wait, Miss Ambrosius." His smirk as he stared at the road was damn near infuriating.

This is not *the kind of surprise I need. Right now, I need zero surprises.*

She pressed her lips together to keep from shouting at him or letting her irritation get the better of her until she did something rash that would put them both in danger inside a moving vehicle. She inhaled deeply and went with using her words instead. "You may not know this about me, but I fucking *hate* that saying."

"Oh, aye? Is that the truth of it?" He chuckled softly, clearly enjoying toying with her while he literally held all control of where they were going and when they would get there in his hands. "So ye're not particularly adept at patience."

"In my experience, the longer I wait, the more screwed-up things tend to get." She shot him a pert look, though there was no telling whether he actually saw it with his gaze glued to the road.

"All right. I've clearly picked the wrong time to add a touch of mystery to our country drive."

"I didn't come here for mystery, Seamus." The words sounded so ridiculous coming out of her mouth that she had to look away from him to hide a smirk. "Well, mostly."

"And not in the form of guessing games, aye. Poor timing on my part." He shot her a playful wink.

Her cheeks flushed again as she quickly returned her attention to the road and tried not to notice. It wasn't from the wink or the man's flirting. It had simply been a long time since she'd had such a blatant reminder of her deeply ingrained tendency to take things too seriously. Even something as playful as riding in a car with Seamus Havalon without any idea where they were going.

You seriously need to lighten up, Halsey. He's a friend, he's helping you when you need help, and you already know you can trust him. Forget everything else.

"Ye asked if I knew such a thing as what's happenin' to ye," Seamus continued gently with amusement still in his voice. "The answer's still no. Unfortunately."

"Uh-huh…"

"But I know a handful of folks who might have a thing

or two to say about it. Can't deny there's plenty o' things they know more about 'n I do, so it can't hurt."

Halsey's smile faded when she realized this wasn't an immediate jump from the harrowing ordeal of telling her most recent magical horror story to a fun and carefree date with a beautiful Irishman. She also realized she wasn't in the mood to be around anyone else right now. Especially if she had to put on a party face for the meet-and-greet that always came first.

"Look, I appreciate everything you're doing and how much you wanna help me right now," she began, trying to keep her voice level and cool. "But I honestly don't feel like meeting a bunch of strangers today, even if there's a chance they—"

A sharp bark of a laugh escaped him, and the car swerved before Seamus managed to gain control. Though his hands quickly steadied on the wheel, he roared with laughter that made Halsey equally concerned.

He's gonna drive us right off the road laughing like that...

Still, his laughter was contagious enough to elicit a confused, medium-sized smile from her. She rolled her eyes and tried to catch his attention with an over-exaggerated sigh. "What is it this time?"

"You…strangers…ha!" He shook his head, blinking furiously and trying to keep his focus on the road. He still hadn't come down from the apparent hilarity of…whatever she'd said that was so damn funny. "How many folks do ye think I know?"

Halsey scoffed. "That feels like a trick question."

"Well, t'wasn't meant as one. I'm not takin' ye ta any strangers, Hal. I'm takin' ye home."

At first, she thought he was joking again with another dose of misdirection. She laughed and rolled her eyes, then realized he was being serious. "Wait, you mean to your family?"

"That's usually who ye find at home, aye." Seamus shot her another playful smile. "And now I see the t'ought of goin' to family fer a bit of advice isn't somethin' that crosses your mind often."

"No. It's not." They sat in silence for another moment as the lush, sprawling green landscape rushing past them on either side. Then she couldn't help but laugh at how uptight she'd been for so long. How easy it was for the elemental sitting beside her to push her buttons, all without even trying. "Next time, maybe just say that."

"Aye. And save us both the confusion."

They shared another round of laughter, and Halsey finally let herself settle back to enjoy the rest of the drive.

He'd hit the nail on the head with his observations. Again. At one point in her life, Halsey's family had been the only resource she'd truly had. The first place she would have gone for help with something as confusing and potentially life-changing as discovering a new type of magic no other elemental in the world possessed. Now, heading back home to speak with any of the Ambrosius Clan was the last place she wanted to be.

Yet she also knew Seamus' family was entirely different. In ways that surprised her, knowing she was headed back to the Havalon Clan estate felt an awful lot like she *was* going home.

CHAPTER SEVEN

Halsey remembered her and Brigham's drive from Faolán's Inn to the Havalon estate being incredibly long the first time they'd made their way out there to meet an elemental Clan their own family hadn't spoken to in decades. Today, that drive should have felt shorter without going out of the way and waiting in the rundown old inn with a silent, red-faced woman behind the bar for their Havalon contact to show himself.

It didn't.

The longer she sat in the passenger seat of Seamus' car, the more time she had to consider the consequences and potential repercussions of meeting with the Havalon Clan. Again.

This time, though, she and Brigham wouldn't be extending an olive branch on behalf of their family, none of whom knew they'd made a second trip to Ireland on their own time and their own dime. This time, she wouldn't be casually sitting down with the leading members of the Havalon Council to warn them of what she and her cousin had found, to ask about silver coffins and changes in magic, or to trade international stories about the rules of magic and monsters.

This time, Halsey would be walking up that front lawn to the sight of familiar faces, to warm embraces and laughter. To the kind of hospitality she knew she would receive from the Irish Clan who'd accepted her with open arms simply because she'd shown up. More than that, the conversation during her second visit wouldn't be so universal, either.

Instead of werewolf problems, monsters ravaging the countryside unchecked, or family feuds now beginning the long road to reconciliation, the topic of conversation would be closer to home.

Halsey would have to tell a few personal stories all over again to get everyone on the same page. She'd have to explain what she'd been trying to accomplish in meeting Hayden. She'd have to show them the copper orb, explain how she'd created it and what it could do, and why it felt infinitely more dangerous to share the truth with her own flesh and blood than with a Clan she'd only seen brief mentions of in her family's historical records.

She'd have to talk about herself.

That had never been part of her comfort zone. Even with Brigham, who'd been her best friend since they were born.

So while Seamus chatted away in the driver's seat, making friendly conversation and subtly preparing her for conversation points with various members of his family, Halsey heard his words. She nodded at all the right moments and smiled when he did. But she wasn't truly listening.

All her attention had been sucked into her growing levels of discomfort at the thought of what she would have to do when they reached the Havalon estate.

Talking about all these things with a single person whose company she enjoyed and whose judgment she trusted, plus a consistent flow of drinks, was one thing.

Forcing herself to calmly and coherently recount the relevant facts with an entire Clan who called her the Alpha Hunter? Who'd ceremoniously *thanked* her for ridding them of their own personal monster problem despite the fact that she and Brigham had made it worse during their last real mission in Ireland that they'd thought they'd completed successfully? That was something else entirely.

Yet she'd gotten into Seamus' car of her own free will. He was naturally calling the shots and had chosen to postpone their date in lieu of bringing her to his family again, and there was nothing she could do about it.

That didn't sit well with her, either.

"Seamus," she muttered, fighting hard to keep both her voice and her energy levels low and even.

After being interrupted by the sound of his name in an unexpectedly serious tone, Seamus chuckled and shot her a quick look. "Uh-oh. I've overwhelmed ye with all the party facts, haven't I? Feel free to take what ye like and leave the rest at the door. It's not like they all don't know who ye are already."

"I don't know if I can do this."

"Oh." He looked at her again, his smile slowly fading with realization. "Well, now I feel like a real eejit, babblin' on like this fer as long as I have. Didn't mean ta go too far with the stories. But ye know my kin anyhow, and they know you. I'm lookin' forward ta—"

"Please stop the car."

"Eh?" Now he frowned at her with multiple doubletakes, confused by the sudden change in her demeanor. "There's nothin' ta worry about, Hal. Trust me."

"I said stop the car!" The shouted command burst from her with far more force than she'd ever wanted to use. Especially with him and especially now. Only after it was out did she realize she'd clenched her eyes tightly shut, as well as her fists. If he hadn't thought she was crazy before, she'd probably changed his mind.

"Aye. Sure." His easygoing smile and pervading playfulness were gone as he calmly decelerated and pulled over. The Volkswagen bumped and wobbled as half the tires left the asphalt for the thick grass of the nonexistent shoulder. Seamus quickly shifted into park, then turned a concerned frown toward her. "Listen, if I said anythin' that—"

Halsey had already whipped off her seatbelt and violently shoved open her door so she could stumble out onto the grass in the warm air of early evening. An overwhelming need to get out, to get as far away as possible from where she was right now, surged through her. She didn't try to fight it.

She stumbled a few times across the grass on legs that didn't seem to want to work the way they were supposed to, but then she gained control and kept walking. Unthinking. Without direction or any idea where she was going other than she couldn't stop because if she did…

If she did, something awful would happen.

"Halsey!" Seamus shouted after her.

She couldn't have gone far into the endless field of green, but his voice sounded so far away. If she could keep moving, she could leave everything else behind and wouldn't have to deal with the consequences of making all the wrong decisions.

"Where in the world d'ye think ye're goin'?" His voice was full of confusion but closer and louder now. "There's nothin' out here fer miles."

Despite the tingling in her hands and feet and the fact that her legs felt like jelly, Halsey kept moving. She couldn't turn to face him because he'd see the tears in her eyes. She had no idea why they were even there.

"Damn it, Hal. Stop runnin' away and bloody *talk* ta me so I can help!"

For some reason, that made her stop. Maybe because Seamus was yelling at her now. It could have been the notes of alarm and concern in his voice or the fact that he thought she was running away from *him.* Which wasn't necessarily untrue but also wasn't the specific reason she'd had to get out of the car. She wanted to run away from everything.

She stood in the grass, yards away from the car on the side of the road, and a sudden wave of nausea nearly crippled her. Maybe it was the four pints at the pub and having eaten nothing else since waking up this morning. Or carsickness. Or the copper orb was turning on her and using her newfound magic to tear her up from the inside now that it had ensnared her the way it had always wanted…

Her hand almost went to her jacket pocket to make sure

the thing was still there, but then she thought she might be sick and immediately doubled over, her hands propped on her thighs. Her eyes burned with tears, and she couldn't see a thing but one blurry stretch of green below her.

Seamus' swishing footsteps grew louder, then he was beside her with a gentle, tentative hand on her back. "You all right, there?"

Her breath heaved in and out of her chest, but she couldn't seem to get enough of it.

"Halsey?" His hand left her back, then he leaned forward to get a good look at her face. "I'd love ta help ya, but I don't know what's happenin'. Can ye maybe give me a bit of a clue here?"

After taking another few deep breaths and realizing she wouldn't be physically sick anytime soon, she swallowed thickly and straightened. She brushed stray hairs away from her face that had already flushed hot and was now slick with sweat. Then she closed her eyes and shook her head. That was all she *could* do.

What the hell's wrong with you, Halsey? Say something. Talk to the guy, for fuck's sake.

She couldn't say anything.

"Is it…" With a sharp, uncertain inhale, Seamus reached toward her shoulder but immediately thought better of it. "Did I do somethin'?"

The words she wanted to say stuck in her throat and nearly made her choke. That this had nothing to do with him, and she didn't even know what was happening. Still, she had to say *something* because this was ridiculous.

Knowing that nothing about this reaction made any sense, she struggled to make her body comply with what felt like two separate entities inside her. When she finally shook her head and managed to form real words in a gravelly rasp, the words themselves had nothing to do with what she'd meant to say.

"I can't do this, Seamus. I shouldn't be here. I shouldn't have gotten on that plane. I should've called Brigham and told him everything, then I should've gone straight home to figure out what the hell's *wrong* with me—"

"Whoa, whoa. Hey, now." This time he did put a hand on her shoulder before stepping in front of her to face her directly.

She clenched her eyes shut again, feeling both ridiculous for acting this way and incapable of stopping it. Tiny, continuous trembles surged through her body, but she wasn't vomiting, and she felt like she could breathe again.

"Will ye look at me?" he asked softly. His other hand settled gently on her other shoulder. Warm, solid, grounding.

She swallowed thickly. She couldn't get sucked into the feeling of his hands or the heat of his body standing so close to her now, smelling like cinnamon and leather and a hint of hops.

Don't say anything else, Halsey. You sound like an idiot, and nobody wants to bring an idiot home to their family.

"Come on, now. Open yer eyes," Seamus prompted one more time. His hands moved slowly up and down her arms like he was trying to rub some life back into them without breaking her. "I promise ye I'm just as handsome as the last time ye looked, so ye needn't worry 'bout any o' *that* changin.'"

The unexpectedly ridiculous words of encouragement

were apparently what was needed to break the spell of whatever awful thing had gripped her. Halsey laughed without realizing it, then her eyes fluttered open.

Seamus chuckled with her as her gaze settled on the middle of his chest instead of his face, but he'd gotten her to open her eyes.

And she'd started breathing normally again, too.

"There ye are." He dipped his head toward her, and she managed to lift her chin enough to look into his sparkling blue eyes. "Feelin' better?" he asked

She blinked back the tears that thankfully hadn't managed to slip their way out, which would have been more embarrassing than she could handle on top of everything else right now. Halsey bit her lower lip and shook her head a fraction of an inch. "Not really. Now I feel like an idiot."

"Nah." Seamus playfully wrinkled his nose, the corners of his eyes crinkling above a growing smile. "I know plenty of eejits, Hal, believe me. Ye're nothin' of the sort. Not even a wee bit."

She had to look away from him then because he was handling this whole thing better than she ever would have been able to if she were in his situation. Halsey had come to Ireland for Seamus' help and to get another perspective on the untamed, almost deadly turn her morning had taken, not to mention her magic. Running wildly through a field in the middle of nowhere and thinking she was losing her mind hadn't been on the itinerary. Nor had fishing for compliments. Yet the only thing she could think of to say was a hollow, murmured, "I have no idea what that was, but…I'm so sorry—"

"Ye can feel sorry all ye want. Hard ta stop ye from doin' anythin' when yer mind's set to it. Clearly."

She released another wry, self-conscious laugh and shook her head because there wasn't anything else she *could* do.

Seamus continued, his hands still stroking her arms as if that had brought her back to her right mind from the start. "For what it's worth, the apology's entirely unnecessary. Because ye have nothin' to apologize *for*. Even if ye don't believe me, which knowin' *ye*, I'm willin' ta bet that's the next stop in your line o' thinkin'."

CHAPTER EIGHT

When she looked up at him again, there was no trace of confusion, malice, or irritation in his features. Merely an open amusement, a warm smile, and a hint of relief that surprised her. "Seamus, I made you stop in the middle of nowhere, then I ran away. From you *and* the car."

He chuckled and dipped his head. "Aye, ye did. And I came after ye. Simple as that."

"This isn't what normal people do after they haven't seen each other for months."

He scoffed and shot a fake exasperated glance toward the clear blue sky, but his smile remained. "If either one of us is tryin' ta be *normal*, knowin' who and what we are and what we do so the rest o' the world doesn't have ta, *then* I'd tell ye we've both got some serious problems ta work out."

"Right." As her pulse settled into something closer to an acceptable rate and the trembling in her body mostly subsided, Halsey was able to smile at that. This whole thing was absurd, but it was happening. Absurdity hadn't ever stopped her before. That didn't mean it was any easier not to let it stop her now. "Well, I don't know about you, but I *do* have a few serious problems. Obviously."

"Oh, aye. Ye've made that abundantly clear." They both laughed, and he studied her face for what felt like an incredibly long time. "Now, if ye'd run out me car screamin' yer head off and sayin' ye never wanted ta see me again, I'd be a wee bit more concerned, sure. But this? T'isn't one of those problems I'm referrin' to. Believe me, this is nothin'."

"Sounds like one of those things that's easier to say than to actually believe, though."

When he ducked his head again and masked his expression from her, Halsey thought she'd said the absolute wrong thing and immediately regretted all of it.

Shit. Not helping.

"Not that I think you're the kind of person who says things for the sake of saying them," she blurted, waiting for him to look at her again. "That's not what I meant. I just—"

Seamus' next deep inhale cut her off, and only then did she realize he'd been silently laughing instead. Her cheeks burned, and she noticed his hands had stopped moving along her arms and had settled comfortably on her shoulders again.

Great. I'm running across fields like a madwoman, rambling my head off, and he's only now *figuring out what he got himself into. It's not gonna last long after this.*

"All right," he finally announced after another soft chuckle. "If I let ye keep talkin' yerself in circles, I might not have a chance ta say much of anythin' else. So can I make a request?"

"A request." Her eyes widened, and she stared at him in

mute surprise before remembering he'd asked her a question. "I mean, sure. Go for it."

"Will ye stop tryin' ta make excuses *against* yerself and just listen?"

"I'm not—" Halsey stopped mid-sentence when amusement flickered across his face, then she clamped her mouth shut and nodded.

He grinned. "Well, that was easier than I expected."

She pursed her lips in mock consternation, which only made his grin widen.

"This feels like somethin' that's needed sayin' fer some time, but more importantly, it's somethin' I think ye need ta hear. So bear with me."

It wasn't the kind of start she'd expected, but she nodded for him to continue. Now it seemed she was about to get one more lecture in the long line of them she'd received in her life. The fact that it was coming from a good-looking Irishman who'd chased her into a field instead of Brigham, Greta, or anyone on her family Council didn't make it more appealing.

But when Seamus' hands moved along her shoulders and down her arms again, the tension in her body started to melt away.

When he reached her forearms and kept going until he was holding both of her hands in his, she swallowed and could do nothing but stare at him.

And now this feels like a confession. Or something else I'm not in the right headspace to hear right now...

"To start, I can fully admit I don't understand what ye're goin' through nearly as much as I wish I did. Ye've told me yer stories. Ye've trusted me with 'em. And I haven't thanked ye for that as I ought ta have. So thank ye."

A small frown flickered across Halsey's brow, and she pressed her lips together to keep from saying anything after having promised she'd shut up and listen.

"What I *do* understand, very well, in fact, is that ye're different, Hal. And no, I'm not only sayin' it 'cause you owe me that dinner." He winked at her, lightening the seriousness of his words enough to make her smile in return. "Ye're stronger'n most. Ye're sharp as a whip, which is hard enough ta find in most people. Add to that ye'll stop at nothin' to get ta the bottom of a thing, no matter how much ye have ta put yerself through or how often ye have ta stand against the folks who *should* be behind ye all the way…"

Then he paused, his eyes briefly narrowing as he studied her face with the barest hint of a frown. Almost like he didn't quite know how to continue the way he wanted.

When Halsey gave his hands an encouraging squeeze, it was without thought and surprisingly without the mental chatter of second-guessing herself.

And it was all he needed.

"Listen, I don't think I'd be wrong in sayin' ye haven't found a place with rest of yer kin, no matter how long 'n how hard ye've been fightin' fer 'em. So it stands ta reason ye'd feel a wee bit squeamish 'bout comin' out here instead of goin' home and layin' yerself bare in front of a family that hasn't spoken ta yers in far too long.

"Now, I'm not sayin' I expect ye ta let me in on all the personal details of it. That's yer business ta share or ta keep however ye please." The warmth of his hands seemed to grow as he slightly tightened his hold on them. He took another step toward her, lifting her hands to his chest until they were all that was left between them.

Halsey had to tilt her head back almost all the way to keep looking up at him, but she didn't pull away. Nor did it occur to her at the moment that she *always* pulled away when someone who wasn't an Ambrosius monster hunter through and through got too close for comfort. Seamus was even closer now, and if she'd had the presence of mind to consider it, she would have realized that for the first time, it didn't bother her in the least.

He continued softly. "What I *can* tell ye is that ye won't be turned away here. Better yet, I can *promise* ye won't. So whatever it is ye're thinkin' that makes ye pause, or want ta pull away, or question whether ye're headin' in the direction ye need ta go, I want ye ta hear there's no need. There never will be. Ye're doin' the right thing, even if it feels like ye've gotten yerself inta the exact opposite. Do ye understand?"

Halsey couldn't look away from his eyes. She couldn't do much of anything but stand there, let him hold her hands, and slowly nod.

With a confused smile, Seamus released one of her hands to reach toward the thick, lush green grass at their feet. She felt something shift in the life force around them. A tiny shiver of magical energy that could only have come from him, though she had no idea what it might be. Honestly, she didn't care.

When he lifted his hand again, he held something in a loosely closed fist and sighed as he looked down at it. "If ye take nothin' else from everythin' I've said, remember this."

The energy shift grew stronger before a small glow of barely visible green light emanated from Seamus' closed fist. It instantly drew her attention, and they watched together as the green light flickered and grew stronger.

"Ye belong here, Hal. Like the rest of us."

Seamus slowly unfurled his fingers as the seed he'd pulled from within the blades of grass sprouted in his palm. In seconds, the sprout opened up, tripled in size, and produced a tiny green bud that bloomed almost instantly into a pale yellow flower.

"And ye always will." He met her gaze, and his playful grin returned. "Whether ye like it or not."

For a few seconds, Halsey looked back and forth between his brilliant grin and the magically blossomed flower resting in his open palm.

Seamus twirled the flower in his fingers, released her other hand, and fluidly tucked the blossom behind her ear to settle against the backdrop of her dark hair. "I do think ye'll get used to it easier'n ye thought."

They stood there in the middle of the field for another long moment, gazing at each other after the masterful little speech he'd given.

She wanted to thank him because he'd been right. It was what she'd needed to hear, even if she hadn't been aware of it until afterward. Yet instead of coming up with something equally meaningful to express her appreciation, she chortled and quipped, "You figured I was the kinda girl who'd be swept off her feet by a pretty flower in her hair?"

He wrinkled his nose in mock uncertainty and tilted his

head as if fully considering the question that wasn't meant to be taken seriously. "Well, I wasn't certain one way or t'other, really." He chucked her softly under the chin with the side of his knuckle and added, "But it suits you."

"Oh, well *played*, Mr. Havalon."

"Much obliged." He gave her shoulders one more reassuring squeeze, then swept an arm toward his car. "I haven't changed my mind 'bout bringin' ya home with me. O' course, we could walk if ye prefer, but it's rather a long way yet. And, ah…" He shot her a playful grimace before nodding at the Volkswagen. "That isn't *technically* my car."

Laughing, Halsey spun around, surprised to find how much ground she'd covered in her mad dash away from the road and whatever else her overloaded subconscious had been trying to put behind her. "The car. Definitely the car. I think we've walked far enough already."

"Aye? Well, that's a relief."

CHAPTER NINE

The remainder of their drive to the Havalon estate lasted half an hour. Their unexpected little pit stop in the middle of nowhere had vastly improved Halsey's mood, making those last thirty minutes fly by more quickly than she would have thought.

Seamus had taken it upon himself to *keep* the mood light and relatively carefree with a consistent stream of friendly chattiness. This time, however, he'd changed the topic of conversation from the projects, missions, and escapades of his family members during the last few months since Halsey and Brigham's first visit. Now, he filled the time with stories about certain members of the Havalon Clan whose phobias, minor neuroses, and incredibly odd quirks had been the topic of family conversation and the source of jokes for years.

Halsey wasn't naïve to the fact that he'd singled out members of his family with particular attributes in a subtle attempt to make her feel more comfortable with her minor episode. Neither of them brought it up again after their joint decision to continue on their way as if nothing had happened.

She appreciated that more than she could put into words.

Seamus' stories were successful at their intended effect, which was to take Halsey's mind off her own troubles for a little while and retrospectively reveal the humor of the human condition, including some of its most uncomfortable parts. He didn't have to reiterate that Halsey had nothing to apologize for or be ashamed of. Yet beneath the surface of his expertly told stories with punchlines in all the right places and accurate impersonations of the Havalons she'd met and remembered, the message was still clear.

If she could laugh her way through what felt like the worst of her problems and the heaviest of her burdens, she'd make it through them all before the end.

It also gave her a new appreciation for Brigham's off-the-cuff humor that occasionally bordered on slapstick. Despite her cousin's fondness for logic and reason, plus his ability to charm and negotiate his way into and out of almost every situation imaginable, Brigham's sense of humor helped him keep going no matter what they faced.

Halsey imagined it was the same for the Havalon Clan, who threw parties in the giant backyard of their own estate nearly every night simply because they enjoyed each other's company. That was a lot easier to do when so many relatives sharing a single enormous home were well-practiced in laughing off their graver concerns. She'd only spent twenty-four hours with them. In that amount of time, she experienced the way those concerns had been openly discussed and shared with honesty and familial trust in the fact that everything would work out as it should.

It was one of the many traits sorely lacking within the Ambrosius Clan as a whole. She didn't see her family making any changes to that particular segment of their MO anytime soon.

Knowing the kind of welcome that awaited her at the Havalon estate also made it a lot easier and less uncomfortable to put aside thoughts of her own family dynamics. Which she would still have to deal with when she returned to their estate outside Lufkin, Texas.

She'd told Brigham that Seamus Havalon had invited her to stay with the Havalons again. As far as any other Ambrosius elemental was concerned, that was exactly what she was doing. Now that the truth had finally caught up with her cover story, it was a relief to recognize she had nothing to feel guilty about because she also had nothing to hide.

For now, while she was in Ireland, anyway. When she went home, it would be a different story. Still, Halsey had thoroughly committed herself to enjoying her time here. She'd let the rest of her worries wait until she could actually address them.

So she laughed along with Seamus as he described his cousin Finn's compulsion to always keep his shoelaces the same length after tying them, his aunt Claire's complete disgust for anything that wasn't perfectly symmetrical, and his other cousin Brennan's inability to manipulate metal compounds into any form beyond the splatter shape of soldered steel on concrete.

With her own intricate knowledge of metalworking and her family's alchemy specialty, Halsey found Brennan's magical frustrations particularly amusing. She didn't offer any commentary because she had a feeling anything she might have said would most likely be used as fuel for more good-natured jokes against the Havalon elementals in question. If her opinions were to be used like that, she'd rather make the joke in person.

She recognized the rise of the last hill they climbed in the Volkswagen as Seamus finished describing his second cousin Thomas' immense and irrational fear of spiders. "Almost ran his own brother through on his way out o' that cave ta get away from the wee things."

They both laughed as the car crested the hill, revealing the view Halsey remembered so well. It had both surprised and charmed her the first time she'd seen the sprawling main house of the Havalon estate surrounded by smaller outbuildings on either side. "That's a pretty common fear, though, isn't it? Of spiders?"

"Not like Thomas', t'isn't. The poor man forgets his own name until he's put five meters between himself and the creepy crawlies."

"So what happens if he finds spiders in the house?"

"Ah. Well, we figured out it's a hell of a way ta get him on his ass when he takes too damn long ta get a move on." Seamus flashed her the mischievous grin she finally thought she was starting to understand and lowered his voice as if they weren't still alone in the car. "Me and a few o' the lads've taken ta handin' out the wee plastic ones ta all the bairns. The kiddos, aye? Christ, he hates it, but there's nothin' like watchin' those young ones fallin' all over themselves with glee when they send him runnin' and screamin' from the big house."

"You know, part of me would actually love to see that. And the other part..."

"Trust me, Hal. Listen ta the other part. It's not a sight ya want burned inta yer mind for the rest o' yer life. If ye can help it, save yerself the trouble."

The dirt road flattened and stretched out ahead of them, cutting straight through the vast swath of open grass leading to the Havalon estate's main house. As Halsey studied the front façade and the squat brown buildings peeking out from behind the big house on either side, an unexpected wave of nostalgia washed over her.

On her last visit, she'd hunted down a wayward werewolf pack, unintentionally killed the werewolf alpha as the man within the monster begged for death, and experienced the agony of having a monster claw embedded in her leg, then subsequently removed by Fiona Havalon's skilled healer's hands. Despite those events, a deeper part of her hadn't wanted to leave this place so soon after she and Brigham had discovered it. The Havalon Clan had told them they were always welcome to return. The Ambrosius cousins had quickly and efficiently become honorary members of a family they'd known about but had never met.

The sight of the big house, the enormous green lawn, and the thick forest behind the property against a mountain backdrop filled her with a surprising level of ease, comfort, and excitement she'd never experienced when pulling onto her own Clan's property. The only place she'd ever felt this kind of belonging without seeing or talking to anyone first was at her own little cottage way back in the middle of the fields on her family's land. She'd always assumed that was because when she was home yet living so far away from the rest of the Clan, she didn't have to deal with people if she didn't feel like it.

This is what coming home is supposed to feel like, isn't it? Not like a militia headquarters or being put on the spot in the Council room. Not being stared at by a bunch of your own flesh and blood who've already made up their minds about how much you've failed...

The thought was so surprising and so dead-on that she barked a laugh before clapping a hand over her mouth.

"What's this, now?" Seamus asked with a crooked smile as the dirt road ended, and he kept driving them onto the wide swath of grass in front of the big house. "I've always thought I've had a fairly sharp wit meself, Hal. But if there's that much of a lag between a little dry humor and gettin' a good laugh or two, maybe I oughta rethink my skillsets."

"Sorry. No, it's not you." She shook her head, her eyes growing wider by the second. A grounded weight of peaceful belonging settling in her chest and over her shoulders like a warm blanket.

"Oof. Sounds like I should *definitely* rethink my skillsets."

"There's nothing wrong with your stories or your jokes, Seamus." She cast him a sidelong glance and a coy smile. "And not everything's about you."

"Ha! Ye know, me ma's been sayin' the same thing fer years."

"Yeah, well, your mom's an incredible woman. Married

into *this* family without a drop of magic in her, and she's somehow managed not to kill any of you."

"Oh, aye, and she can patch ye up from just 'bout anythin' faster'n ye can say, '*Shite*, that hurts!'"

With her good mood restored and further buoyed by returning to the home of the elemental family who'd accepted her far more gracefully than her own, Halsey's laughter came easily now. It helped that Seamus making good-natured fun of his mother as the Clan's in-house healer was closer to the truth than most other jokes could get. Fiona Havalon was capable of incredible things when her particular healing skills were in high demand, and Halsey had experienced it firsthand.

Finally, the Volkswagen rolled to a stop in the grass among all the other Havalon vehicles parked however their drivers saw fit at the moment. Seamus turned off the ignition, then shifted in his seat to meet her gaze directly. A curious smile played on his lips as he looked between Halsey's profile and the front of his family's home.

"So what is it, then?" he asked, raising his eyebrows.

"What's what?" she responded absently, drinking in the vision of the first physical place to have stolen her heart in under twenty-four hours. She simply couldn't look away.

"What is it that's got ye lookin' all starry-eyed and giddy, eh? If there was a good-lookin' fella standin' there in front o' the car, it'd make a lot more sense. Granted, I'd have ta rethink my strategy for keepin' yer attention, but at least I'd understand." He grinned and gestured toward the wide house cutting the flat expanse of open Irish meadow. "But *this* is only a buildin'."

"I know."

They sat there another moment in silence, then Seamus clicked his tongue. "All right, well, it might be a wee bit too late fer askin' a question o' this sort, but I won't feel right 'til it's outta the way, so... Ye're not secretly one o' those kinda folks who fall in love with inanimate objects instead of people, are ye?"

Halsey pressed her lips together to keep the smile off her face and tore her gaze from the Havalon big house. She fixed Seamus with a deadpan stare and raised an eyebrow. "You've heard the saying, 'There's no such thing as a stupid question,' right?"

"Aye, sure."

With a curt nod, she blinked and added, "That was the exception."

Seamus laughed and spread his arms with a sheepish shrug. "I had ta ask…"

"No, you didn't."

"Hey, it's a real thing, Hal. Haven't ye heard the stories? Matter o' fact, there was another one in the papers a few weeks past. Happens all the time, apparently."

Exaggerating a throat-clear so she wouldn't end up encouraging his ridiculous line of questioning, she unbuckled her seatbelt and opened the passenger-side door in one swift movement. "I'm getting out of the car now."

She didn't wait for him to respond or even climb out with her. When she was on her feet again, she gently closed the door and headed for the far-left side of the big house, which was the same route she and Brigham had followed Brigham along during their last visit.

"I'm thrilled ta see how happy ye are ta be back here," he

called after her before the echoing thump of the driver-side door closing sounded. "But ye still haven't answered the question."

"And I never will," she called over her shoulder without fully looking back at him.

His laughter was the only reply before the swift rustle and thud of his loping strides as he half-jogged after her to catch up. When he reached her side, Seamus gently elbowed her shoulder and murmured, "I feel the same way drivin' across this field, ye know."

"Like *you* might be in love with a house?"

"Ye're very clever." They both laughed as they kept walking, cutting diagonally from the informal grass parking lot for the hedges growing along the left outer wall of the big house. "It's the feelin' of a good home."

Halsey sighed in mock relief and playfully rolled her eyes. "I'm so glad you're saying things that actually make sense again."

"Aye?"

She shrugged and looked up at the overhanging eaves scattered with twiggy birds' nests above freshly stained, rich dark brown shutters against the slightly lighter taupe of the exterior siding. "I know what you mean about the feeling of a good home, though. I guess I didn't understand what that was until a few minutes ago."

"That's the thing, isn't it? Once ye know a feelin' fer what it is, there's no goin' back."

She looked up at him with a playful frown. "Back to what?"

Seamus strolled casually along beside her. His hands slid into the front pockets of his jeans as he absently scanned the outbuildings coming into view and the edge of the tree line at the back of the Havalon's enormous yard. "To what it felt like *before* ye realized what was missin'."

Halsey tilted her head in consideration. Once again, he'd nailed the feeling she'd been struggling to name. Almost as if he'd already been through it himself. Or as if he could read her mind, which wasn't possible.

"Huh." Seamus chuckled as they rounded the front corner. "Sounds rather lovely when it's put that way, doesn't it?"

"Almost like you've been through the exact same thing…"

"Aw, o' course not. Not *exactly* the same, anyhow. It's more like the two of us're movin' through it at the same time, only I might be a smidge keener'n ye are ta think it through out loud."

She wrinkled her nose and choked back a laugh at his sheepish smile bordering on a grimace. "You see how it's hard to believe you're realizing all this for the first time when you're the one who grew you up here, right?"

"Aye, o' course. It's the same feelin', though." She clearly wasn't buying his explanation. He rubbed the back of his neck and studied the slowly expanding view of the giant back lawn as they passed the hedges. "We're just comin' at it from different sides, is all."

"How do you mean?"

He offered a carefree shrug and sighed. "My home's always been right here, aye. But the place didn't feel the same after ye left a few months back, and I couldn't pin down *what* it was. It was only after I watched ye hop out the car and head this way that I realized what's been missin' since."

Halsey beamed and quickly dipped her head to hide the reaction she had no control over.

Okay, he gets credit for knowing how to pull the right strings. The guy's got serious game. If I'm not careful, I might believe it enough that I don't ever leave.

She chuckled at the thought, and Seamus dipped his head to catch her gaze.

"Ye find that part funny, do ye?"

"Not *funny*, no. It's just... I wasn't even here for a full twenty-four hours last time."

"Aye. I remember." When he met her gaze again, his smile wasn't nearly as strong or as playful as it had been a moment before. If Halsey didn't know better, she would have thought he looked embarrassed. "But it was all *ye* needed ta understand ye'd found the thing ye never quite knew was missin'."

Damn it, he's right...

She stopped walking and stared up at him with wide eyes, not quite daring to believe he might have meant every word. The part of her that had always been wary of getting close to people in general, that hadn't been remotely interested in dating anyone when there were monsters to hunt and missions to complete, wanted to laugh it all off and say something witty to defuse the tension.

That part of her was at a complete loss for words.

Seamus scanned the edge of the backyard as if he'd fully expected her skepticism and wasn't fazed by it. "Ye may be quite a bit better at most things than most other people,

Hal. But I'm fairly certain that doesn't apply to some sort o' minimum timeframe fer a person knowin' how they feel."

His blue eyes trailed slowly back toward her, sparkling with amusement and a playfulness that didn't match the flicker of a smile at one corner of his lips.

Almost like he was daring her to argue with him.

There's no way to argue with something like that. So what the hell am I supposed to do with it now?

In the stretching silence, she swallowed thickly and ducked her head, hoping it looked more like she was acknowledging his point than just giving up for the sake of not arguing. "You're right. I'm sorry."

Seamus nodded, pressing his lips together and stealing sidelong glances at her as if he was waiting for a second part to her apology.

A self-conscious chuckle escaped her. "Honestly, I don't know why I'm still so surprised by the way you put words to what most people can't."

Fortunately, going with the truth instead of whatever she thought he wanted to hear was the right decision. He rocked back on his heels, then flashed a grin before pretending to be serious again. "Sorry ta burst yer bubble."

"Hey, it's good to do every once in a while. I won't hold it against you."

"I honestly wouldn't mind it even if ye did." His smile grew as he bit his lower lip and studied her face. Then Seamus chuckled and shook his head. "Look at us. Standin' here by the shrubbery like we're afraid ta get caught."

"I never said I was afraid."

He laughed and grabbed her hand so quickly and casually that Halsey didn't realize what he'd done until he was pulling her along. She laughed with him because what else could she do?

"Come on. If I timed it right, we'll catch 'em before they're too hammered ta believe what they're seein'."

"Oh, sure. Of course. Timing." They passed the first few outbuildings that created the relatively circular perimeter of the back lawn, and Halsey struggled not to rip her hand away and rush in front of him toward the warm welcome she knew they were about to receive. "What exactly are they gonna be seeing?"

Seamus slowed a little, then laughed sheepishly. "Right. I suppose it slipped my mind ta tell ya on the way."

"Tell me what, Seamus?"

His grin returned full force, and he nodded toward the rows of picnic tables set up in the middle of the grass before tugging her along again. "They had no idea ye'd be here."

CHAPTER TEN

Before they'd made it more than a few yards past the far end of the big house, the sounds of yet another enormous Havalon Clan nightly get-together already echoed their way toward the two young elementals. Halsey's cheeks hurt from grinning at the familiarity of walking into this yard again to the same sight as the first time.

Children ran barefoot across the grass, screaming and laughing and twirling around each other as they ducked and weaved between the gathered adults. Banquet tables lined up along the back of the big house, covered in platters piled high with summer evening fare. Basically, it amounted to anything a hungry person could imagine.

Groups of Havalon elementals stood around the yard with drinks in hand, regaling each other with stories and laughing uproariously. A woman Halsey didn't remember meeting last time poked her head out of the big house's rear doors to scowl at the children and snap, "If ye can't keep yerselves away from that table, I swear on each o' yer ma's heads I'll do it for ye. And ye best believe ye won't be likin' how I manage it!"

Some of the kids with a bit more speed and experience darted away from the picnic table in question, scattering like bowling pins with wide eyes and wordless shouts of alarm. The younger ones, or those who hadn't quite learned their lesson about the worst times to *not* take their elders seriously, spun to eye the woman with dubious frowns and zero intentions of obeying. A few of them even egged each other closer to the table to test their elders' limits.

Those were the kids unfortunate enough to receive the full brunt of the shouting Havalon woman's irritation.

With a hiss, she tossed a hand toward the half-dozen young ones who hadn't immediately heeded the warning. Green light bloomed across the grass, zigzagging like slow-motion lightning bolts. At least, slow for lightning. It was incredibly fast for both elemental magic and the extent of certain Havalon children's reflexes.

When the light reached the children, bright green vines and writhing tree roots shot up from beneath the earth with surprisingly quiet *pops* and little to no dirt tossed. The roots twined themselves around a chubby little ankle, a curiously outstretched hand, or a wriggling body that couldn't stand the thought of *not* investigating the one thing they had been told to avoid.

In seconds, all six disobedient little elementals were whisked off their feet and into the air. The brilliant green vines coiling around their heads, necks, and mouths, gently enough not to cause any harm but tightly enough to make effective gags, muted their cries of disappointment and frustration.

The other children who'd managed to escape this cringe-worthy fate watched with wide eyes from the safety of the sidelines. A trio of teenagers lying in the grass with open books looked up and sniggered. None of the other adults seemed to pay attention to the method of discipline that would have been highly unorthodox and probably even worthy of outrage among human families.

Even the group of adults sitting at the off-limits picnic table, which was also the only table on the back lawn with every available seat taken, continued with their conversation as if nothing out of the ordinary had occurred to interrupt them.

Then the defiant young Havalons were whisked across the yard toward the open door at the back of the big house, where the vines and tree roots deposited them one by one, on their feet and unharmed, in front of the woman whose job it was to keep them all in line.

"Aw, man..."

"No fair. How come everyone else gets ta see?"

"Ye never let us do *anythin'* fun."

"How come Aldous gets ta keep playin'? If I can't stay, *he* can't stay!"

The woman hissed like she was trying to shoo feral cats away from the back stoop. "Not anot'er word outta any o' ye's. Ye've had yer chance. Up ta yer rooms nah. Gricia's waitin', and she's expectin' a gaggle o' good little bairns to help her turn down the beds."

"It's bedtime *already*?"

"Well, t'will be once ye finish yer chores."

"No..."

"But it's not even *dark* outside—"

"Niamh Brigid Havalon." The woman stuck both hands on her hips and glowered down at the little girl of five, who'd folded her arms in as much defiance as she could muster. "I'm well aware o' the difference 'tween light 'n dark. There'll be no lessons comin' from *ye* tonight. Especially if'n ye're keen ta keep yerself outta the creek when the older boys go fishin' in the morn."

The girl swiveled her head back and forth with an astounding level of attitude that was comical for anyone watching the scene. Not so much for the other children or the woman tasked with keeping them all in line. "Maybe I *fancy* the creek."

"Then maybe ye'll *fancy* wakin' afore dawn tomorrow and spendin' all day with yer cousins, learnin' ta hold yer tongue and do as ye're told. Now every last one o' ye, get ta marchin' this instant. Right up those stairs, 'n I don't wanna hear another word. Gricia either. Shoo."

With dejected sighs, eye rolls, and an especially spiteful glare from young Niamh, the half-dozen children shuffled into the big house and disappeared.

The entire thing lasted a matter of seconds, and it was such an unusual part of the Havalon Clan activities that even Seamus had stopped in his tracks, his fingers still absently intertwined with Halsey's, to watch the commotion in confused disbelief.

When it was over, the woman in the doorway sighed and shook her head. She returned her attention to the limp vines and tree roots resting in scattered coils where they'd dropped the little ones off in front of the door. Clicking her tongue, she flicked her fingers at the motionless vegetation as if she were flinging water droplets over the sink instead of magic over an elemental's tools of discipline.

The dozens of other Havalons on the back lawn continued with their evening as if this was the most ordinary thing in the world.

It didn't seem ordinary to Halsey. She'd instantly picked up on the stark contrast between the stricter corralling of children tonight and the easygoing, laid-back, joyous freedom of an evening at the Havalon estate she and Brigham had walked into months ago.

The unexpected interruption to the celebratory air, combined with the swift and firm removal of the youngest children who couldn't follow the new rules, had her chuckling before she squeezed Seamus' hand to get his attention. "I think I get what you mean now when you said things haven't been the same around here."

Blinking as if she'd ripped him from a dream, he shot her a sidelong glance before sweeping his gaze across the lawn. His lips twitched like they wanted to smile, but the new frown darkening his features seemed to make it impossible. "Aye. I was talkin' 'bout somethin' awfully specific back there, but it certainly didn't include any o' *this*."

"Oh." That was all she could think of to say because now it looked like something even more unusual was at play here. To Halsey, everything about the way this Clan lived their lives and performed their duties as monster hunters was unusual. Yet this particular situation had stretched far beyond the norm, even for the Irishman at her side who'd spent his whole life here.

"Somethin's off," Seamus murmured before nodding toward the woman standing in the open door. "Come on."

Halsey was happy to follow his lead on this one, but it surprised her when he chose to head not toward the woman but one of the other pockets of adults dotting the yard, talking and laughing and picking at their meals from paper plates in their hands.

The closest group saw them almost immediately, and a skinny man in his mid-twenties with a shock of red curls broke away from the conversation to spread his arms and fix Seamus and Halsey with a dazzling grin. "Well, if t'isn't the wayward apple of our eye returned to rub it all in our faces!"

The others in the group turned to see what the heck he was talking about, and they broke out in similar smiles when they recognized who had joined them for the evening.

"Not sure what ye mean by that," Seamus replied with a chuckle. "Whatever ye're expectin' ta be rubbed in your face, I recommend asking someone else to do the honors for you. It's hard enough looking at you without having to touch."

The Havalons in the group burst out laughing, the redheaded man most animatedly of all. He dropped his nearly empty plate on top of the food piled on his neighbor's plate, then strode toward Seamus and Halsey with his arms wide in invitation. "Can't blame you for keeping your distance. It's hard to get enough of this, I know."

When Seamus slid his hand from Halsey's to greet various relatives that were still hard to keep track of on her second visit, she stood back with an expectant smile and slid her hands into her jacket pockets. The cool, smooth surface of the copper orb in her right pocket suddenly beneath her fingers almost made her whip her hand out in alarm, but she pulled herself together.

It's the same thing you've been carrying around for months, Halsey. That hasn't changed. What harm can it do here anyway? The only thing it's ever done for humans *is save their lives.*

She didn't have much time to consider her strange new reaction to the sphere or the fact that she'd nearly forgotten about its existence already. The laughter and brusque embracing between Seamus and his redheaded cousin had come to an end. Which meant Halsey was the natural next target for all their attention.

"Halsey Ambrosius." The redhead awkwardly clapped a hand on the significantly taller Seamus' shoulder.

Halsey grinned back at him. "Ganan."

"How the hell are ye?"

"Better now that I'm here."

Seamus' older cousin Seersha casually popped a grape into her mouth and tried to keep a straight face. "That's all you have ta say? *Better?*"

"It's the short version." Halsey nodded at the woman and shrugged. "If I went with the long version every time someone asked, I'd be here for a week."

They all laughed at that, nodding and tossing back more of their drinks and shooting Seamus knowing smiles of silent approval.

"I know at least one fella who'd be happier'n a pig in shite ta keep ye here that long." Ganan laughed and shook Seamus' shoulder before releasing him.

The much taller, far sturdier son of the Havalon Clan's

Council head took the whole thing in stride. He dipped his head and smiled at Halsey while the redhead jostled him as much as a stiff breeze moved a tree.

"But ye're here now!" Ganan continued. "Which means ye can't stay away, obviously."

"Obviously," Seamus' cousin Clancy echoed, his wildly thick mutton chops bouncing as he spoke around a mouthful of food.

"And we couldn't be happier," Seersha added with a growing smile. She handed her plate to Clancy, who'd already taken on the burden of Ganan's empty plate. "Ye'll have to forgive these daft-headed Neanderthals, Halsey. They've had enough drink ta make 'em dumb but unfortunately not nearly enough ta make 'em shut up."

The guys pretended to be offended while everyone laughed, and Halsey pulled her hands from her pockets to accept Seersha's warm embrace. The first of what she assumed would be many, maybe more than the last time she was here.

"So what're ye doin' on this side o' the pond?" Ganan asked, then immediately pulled a double-take at Seamus before snorting and punching the taller man in the arm. "Besides this hulking lout, o' course."

Seersha *tsked* and shot him a condescending glare. "Go get another drink, Ganan. Better yet, don't come back 'til ye've had three."

"Oh, come on. It's obvious as hell, isn't it? I'm not allowed ta ask reasonable questions?"

"What ye're doin' is makin' an arse of yerself by askin' all the questions nobody wants ta answer." The woman gave Halsey a sympathetic smile, then leaned toward her and winked. "But ye already know not ta listen to at least half of these eejits who *claim* they're related ta those of us with our heads fully screwed onto our shoulders, don't ye?"

Clancy snorted before tearing off half a dinner roll between his teeth. "Some of 'em screwed more tightly 'n others."

"Oh, piss off."

Everyone laughed again, including Halsey and Seamus, though he looked much more distracted by the state of affairs across the lawn, making it impossible for him to be fully present. No one else had seemed to notice his lack of attention, though. They were apparently all too excited to see Halsey again.

After glaring sarcastically at Seersha, Ganan approached Halsey and stopped two feet in front of her before spreading his arms. Then he met Halsey's gaze and smirked. "Can I hug ye? Or is that as off-limits as anything else I might ask?"

"As long as you're not contagious, I guess it's fine."

Clancy and Seersha cracked up laughing, and Ganan sprang forward to wrap her in an astonishingly crushing hug for how skinny he was.

Halsey grunted in surprise and wasn't quite able to hug him back before he released her, but laughing along with everyone else came easily enough.

When he released her, Ganan shot her a quick wink and wagged a finger at her. "I liked ye before, and I might even like ye better now. So remember, if things don't work out between ye and this lumberin' beast over here..." He stuck a thumb toward Seamus, but before he could finish his thought, Seersha slapped his hand away with a condescending scoff.

"Have ye gone daft all over?"

"What?" With a shrug, Ganan offered a sheepish smile. "No harm in tellin' her *I'm* on the market."

"Ye're always on the market."

He rolled his eyes, and Clancy released a deep, rumbling chuckle as he shoveled a massive forkful of freshly sliced baked ham into his mouth. "And no one's buyin'."

"Ye hear this, Seamus?" Ganan smacked his cousin's arm with the back of a hand. "Ye hear the way they treat me when ye're not around?"

"We treat ye the same whether he's back home or not," Seersha cut in. "It's the shite in yer mouth needs cleanin' out."

"Ye're just gonna let her go on like that, are ye?" Ganan nudged Seamus with an elbow, pulled a ridiculous face at Seersha that was better suited for children when the adults' backs were turned, then grinned at Halsey. "Tell ye what. This guy right here used ta be me own personal champion back in the day. Kept the rest o' the monsters from pickin' on me and kept everybody fair."

"Aye." Clancy swallowed thickly and spared his redheaded cousin a glance before diving back into his food. "A regular damsel in distress, ye were."

Seersha snorted as Halsey bit back a laugh. Ganan tilted his head toward Seamus, waiting for some form of response. When none came, he turned fully toward his cousin and socked Seamus in the arm for real this time.

"What the bloody hell's the matter with ye, lad? Feckin' *say* somethin'!"

Seamus reacted to his cousin's unrestrained punch in the arm like it was a fly zipping past his head, but he chose that moment to join the conversation again. Sort of.

"Why's Helena so fashed 'bout keepin' the bairns from the table?"

"Helena." Ganan blinked up at the tall, dark-haired Havalon who truly didn't look anything like him and scoffed. "*Helena?* Fer the love of ev'rthin' good in this world, Seamus, don't tell me ye're more caught up in Helena and the wee ones than all the good standin' right here in front o' ye."

"Oh, bollocks." Seersha rolled her eyes. "If he's talkin' 'bout himself, I'll stab out me own eye."

Clancy looked between her and Ganan and added, "If he's talkin' 'bout himself, I'll stab out *his* eye."

"Tongue might be better, now that ye mention it."

"Or both."

After staring at Seamus for a moment longer, Ganan puffed out an exaggerated sigh, then vigorously scratched his head until his mop of thick red curls nearly stood on end. "I need another drink."

He cut a direct path across the grass toward the open rear door of the house, breaking through his exasperated façade to shoot Halsey another wink and whisper as he passed her, "Good ta have ya back at the madhouse."

None of his cousins paid any attention to his absence, though Seersha shook her head and laughed wryly. Then she noticed Seamus still studying the scene on the lawn as if he were trying to complete a word puzzle in a foreign language and decided to put him out of his misery. "Council's havin' a *cruinniú*, Seamus. Can't leave the bairns ta muck it up as they please."

"A *cruinniú*?" Seamus turned to frown at his cousin. "We don't hold meetin's for Council business in the yard."

"Aye, but it's not like they had much time ta plan for it," Seersha added. "Supper was ready, the whole family came out ta eat, and who d'ye think's left over after that ta set up a private room with all the pomp and circumstance ta go with it? Nah, might as well hold it right out here, smack-dab in the middle of t'all for everyone ta see."

Seamus shook his head, looking more and more baffled by the second. "What's it about?"

"How should *we* know?" Clancy finished stabbing up another massive forkful and paused with it halfway to his mouth, shrugging. "*Ye're* the one with his folks runnin' the show."

"Shite." Seamus grimaced as he scanned the yard again, his gaze returning over and over to the crowded table everyone else was leaving well enough alone.

Halsey tried to follow his gaze, but it was impossible to get a read on what he was thinking and why. To her, it looked like everything on the Havalon estate was fine, albeit stricter on the childcare than she remembered. But *this* elemental family's protocol for handling concerning situations hadn't yet been explained or revealed to her.

Doesn't matter whether I know what a cruinniú *is or not. He wouldn't be looking like he's about to tear somebody apart if everything was peachy around here. Something's definitely wrong.*

After fighting an obvious mental battle with himself for

a moment longer, Seamus sucked on his teeth in aggravation and grimaced. "Why the hell would they call a *cruinniú* without tellin' me a thing 'bout it?"

"They wouldn't." When he turned his disapproving frown onto Seersha, she nodded gently toward the table in question and shrugged. "Yer folks aren't the ones who called it."

Clancy unleashed a startlingly loud belch that echoed across the yard. Several of the children laughed and pointed while a handful of adults turned from their own private conversations to make sure the sound hadn't signaled some form of emergency. A handful of them smiled and gestured toward Halsey standing there with Seamus, but then Clancy grabbed her focus again with his next words. "Ye must know we're thrilled ta see ye here again, Halsey. Now or whenever ye feel like stoppin' by."

Seamus scowled down at his cousin, who wasn't that much shorter than him, unlike the rest of their family. The other Havalon wasn't paying attention.

Clancy held Halsey's gaze instead and shrugged. "But it looks like ye picked a hell of a night ta come back."

She tried to smile as she looked at Seamus, who was still glaring at his cousins as if this was all one big joke and he was not a fan. "Why's that, exactly?"

"Only that ye're not the only person from far away walkin' up ta the Havalons' front door this evenin'."

CHAPTER ELEVEN

Halsey didn't know how to respond to that nugget of information because she had no idea how the Havalon Clan generally responded to visitors other than herself and Brigham. She'd assumed everyone who stepped foot on the Clan's estate property was as welcomed and well-received as they had been months ago, but the current mood seemed to dictate otherwise.

It made her wonder what would have happened if she and Brigham had shown up without Seamus inviting them and guiding them around for introductions first.

Seamus clearly hadn't expected to hear there were other non-Havalons on the property tonight, either. His mouth popped open like he wanted to start screaming at his cousins. He glanced at Halsey and he managed to wrangle his anger enough to continue speaking with relative calm. "That's impossible."

Seersha pursed her lips to the side. "Eh…not tonight, t'isn't."

"Aye? Ye mean ta tell me someone else showed up

without warning, out of the blue, called a *cruinniú*, and the Council dropped everythin' to do so? Just like that?"

She turned her head to look at him, having to crane her neck to even make it possible. "I don't *mean* ta tell ye a thing, Seamus. I'm sayin' that's what happened. Ye might do well ta remember the only folks makin' the real big decisions're the folks sittin' at that table. Not us. So if ye feel like callin' me a liar, that's all well and good s'long as ye fetch us all a round o' drinks in the process, aye? Maybe *two* fer yerself."

The woman looked unfazed by Seamus' anger. Even her reference to being called a liar, which he hadn't explicitly done, was delivered off-handedly. As if she were telling him a stack of mail with his name on it awaited him inside the big house.

Clancy kept munching away at his dinner, oblivious to the rising tension as if this kind of thing happened all the time.

Halsey watched the entire interaction from the sidelines. Part of her was relieved she wasn't more involved, and the other part wished she knew what was going on right now so she could help Seamus the way his cousins didn't seem particularly interested in doing.

Seamus eyed his cousins warily, then closed his eyes to take a deep breath and regroup. "If either of ye can only tell me *one* useful thing, without muddying it up any further'n ye already have, please tell me ye bloody know who's sittin' at that table."

"Foreigners," Clancy muttered without breaking eye contact with his dinner.

"*Elemental* foreigners," Seersha specified, raising her

eyebrows to add to the air of mystery that didn't need adding to.

As soon as the words were out, Halsey's stomach folded in on itself until it sank to the bottom in a tight not.

No way. That's impossible. They would never...

Stunned, she automatically looked at Seamus, partially to gauge his reaction and partially in a silent plea for help. For what, she didn't know.

Apparently, he'd had the same thought. "Did ye know anythin' 'bout yer own family comin' out here?"

A choked laugh escaped instead of the words she intended, and she wondered if the shock of it had made her lose her voice.

Clancy swallowed thickly and cleared his throat. "It isn't *her* Clan," he murmured between more bites of food.

Halsey held Seamus' gaze, slowly shook her head, and managed to croak out, "That'd never happen. Not in a million years."

Clancy waved a flippant hand before bringing it back down to his plate for the other half of his roll. "It's t'other one."

Seamus rolled his eyes. "Other *what*?"

Seersha sighed in exasperation. "Did ye have ta *smoke* somethin' afore comin' back home for the first time in weeks? T'other *Clan*, Seamus."

"Wait, the Grendiers?" Halsey asked in disbelief.

"If that's what they're called, then aye. 'Tis the only other one as far as I know. Unless ye're fixin' ta tell me someone dug up another while the rest of us weren't lookin'."

Seamus dropped his head into his hand to rub his forehead. His eyes clenched tightly shut as he tried to work out why this would happen.

Halsey was still stuck on the fact that the third and final elemental Clan who still existed in the world had been referred to in relevant conversation. By name.

She glanced between Seamus' cousins. Even in her bafflement, she was aware of how ridiculous she must look when her own face warred between bursting with laughter and scowling at them for their attempts to pull off one seriously unfunny practical joke. Except it didn't feel like a joke. It wasn't particularly funny, either.

"Hold on." She held up both hands, hoping that would keep anyone else from immediately interrupting her. "You guys know the Grendiers?"

"What's all the fuss if we did?" Seersha shot her a confused smile. "*Ye're* the one callin' 'em by name."

"Of *course* I know the name of the only other elemental Clan on Earth," Halsey quipped, still too stunned to maintain control of her tone the way she would have liked. "Seems like a pretty fucking important detail when there are only three elemental families left, but hey. I guess we all have different priorities."

Seersha didn't take offense to her suddenly caustic attitude and assume any perceived insults were fully intended, the way nearly anyone in Halsey's family would have if she'd been having this conversation with them instead. Instead, she widened her eyes and looked at Seamus again before a laugh burbled up her throat. "Bloody spitfire, this one, isn't she?"

"I'm sorry," Halsey quickly added, her cheeks flushing

as the stone in her gut kept sinking lower. "That was out of line—"

"Halsey, darlin', I'll stand behind ye in *that* line any day o' the week." Seersha's grin made her feel better, but not much. "I've been feelin' like the only one with any brains around here for longer'n I care ta admit."

"Says more 'bout her than yerself," Clancy offered with another shrug.

"Aye, maybe." The woman turned toward him and crisply tilted her head in challenge. "But ye had just as much trouble with their name, didn't ye?"

"None of *us* have met 'em," Seamus intervened, gazing directly at Halsey now while his cousins took their own thread of the conversation in a different direction. "I do know some of the older folks on our Council have had a dealin' or two with the Grendier Clan from time to time. My folks included, but that must've been…longer ago'n the last time we had an Ambrosius at our hearth. Before ye and yer cousin, I mean."

"Right. Okay." Nodding, Halsey steeled herself enough to turn away from their small group and peek at the only picnic table filled with people. They sat solemnly with their heads slightly bowed, some with drinks in hand, all oblivious to the noise and activity that was normally so much more lively than this.

She thought she could make out Cillian Havalon's broad back and shoulders, almost as wide as his son's. Both he and Seamus stood out among their family *because* of their size. No one else was immediately recognizable, and it was impossible to tell from a distance whether she was scrutinizing a Havalon or a Grendier.

"Did anyone say a thing 'bout why they're here?" Seamus asked.

Clancy offered a noncommittal grunt.

"Well, they couldn't very well go runnin' to the Ambrosius Clan now, could they?" Seersha snorted, then flashed Halsey another wide grin. "No offense."

"Hey, I get it. People have their reasons for not liking my family. Including me." The words had been bitter on her tongue, but upon emerging, they'd fully adopted the casual, joking air that tinged nearly everything Seamus and his family said. Even if they were talking about serious matters that generally lacked humor and levity. Like their current conversation, for one.

If there's anyone I can talk to about my own Clan seriously screwing up over the last decade or two, maybe even longer, it's this family. I already told them more than enough the last time I was here, and now...

"Whatever it is, though. It can't be good, right?"

"More often 'n not, aye." Seamus grimly nodded as he stared at the table where the Havalon Clan's Council members were sitting down with who they now knew were representatives of the Grendier Clan. "Usually, that's what brings folks here in the first place."

It didn't escape Halsey's notice that his words applied to her and Brigham too.

When they'd come here previously, Brigham had reached out to the few contact numbers he'd had for their elemental counterparts in Ireland. Seamus was the one who'd shown up to meet with them. Not particularly because he was interested in what they had to say or thought he could help but because the rest of his Clan had decided not to reply or intervene. Halsey and Brigham were Ambrosiuses, and what good had come from interacting with their family in the last several decades?

Their first visit had checked off several oddly related boxes. Meeting a new elemental family, swapping stories, and banding together at the last minute to march up into the mountains for a hunt.

Cornering and eradicating the silverback werewolf alpha, her first real kill up close and personal despite all Halsey's attempts *not* to end the life of the man named Rolfr Magnusson trapped within the wolf, hadn't been part of the original agenda. Yet that night's events had all been wrapped together, and they'd led directly to more missing and hidden proof that the Mother of Monsters *had* returned.

And discovering that her family had been keeping so many things from her for almost her entire life.

Even then, the Havalons hadn't done a thing to modify their nightly celebrations with two unexpected Ambrosius visitors at their doorstep. Now, young and defiant children were being magically ushered indoors, and the Havalon Clan Council was taking time from their celebratory evening to hold a private *cruinniú* in a relatively public way. Halsey assumed it was their version of an emergency Council meeting. Which meant tonight was a different situation.

Probably even more urgent and more time-sensitive than all the questions Halsey and Brigham had brought to Ireland with them the first time.

All this flashed through her mind in an instant after Seamus' words brought it to her attention. Then Halsey forced herself to look away from the picnic table and turn to meet his gaze.

A silent understanding passed between them, from one rebellious child of a Clan Council member to another.

"What do you need me to do?" she asked.

Seamus nodded, his anger and frustration visibly melting away when he realized Halsey was equally as dedicated to standing beside him as he was to her. The ghost of a smile flickered at one corner of his mouth. "Stay with me."

"Should be easy enough."

"What the bloody hell is this?" Seersha asked incredulously, looking back and forth between them. "The two o' ye's concoctin' some grand scheme all without sayin' a word. Ha!" She looked over her shoulder at Clancy, who somehow managed to have a disproportionately large amount of food on his plate for how consistently he'd been stuffing his face. "Are ye seein' this, Clancy? Tell me ye're seein' this."

"I can see it," he replied without looking up from his food. "None o' my business. None o' yers, either."

"Well, *ye're* no fun tonight." She stared at him for a moment as he kept eating, then scoffed and rolled her eyes. "Seamus, whatever ye're thinkin' 'bout stirrin' up here, and I know ye are, that's yer business. But I still feel compelled to…"

Seersha turned to hopefully pin her other cousin with a warning look. But when she turned back to where his face had been, she found nothing but the golden glow of a sunset filling the sky above the backdrop of the big house. Halsey was gone too.

"Seamus?"

Seersha scanned the enormous back lawn, looking for her cousin's ridiculous height, which was a lot easier than searching for a young woman in her early twenties who could have passed for a full-blooded Havalon with her dark hair and petite frame. She finally spotted Seamus headed for the table where the Havalon Council held their *cruinniú* with their Grendier visitors with Halsey at his side.

"Oh, Christ." Seersha widened her eyes as Seamus stopped their uncle Rafer, also on his way toward the picnic table with a stack of plastic cups in one hand and a large, unopened bottle of liquor in the other. "Clancy," she urged.

Her perpetually hungry cousin grunted behind her before slowly shuffling forward to stand at her side, his eyes not once leaving his plate.

"Ye should go say somethin' to him," she added before squinting and leaning slightly forward as if the motion would help her overhear Seamus and Rafer's conversation.

"Piss off," Clancy grumbled.

"Oh, aye?" She turned toward him with a pert frown. "That's how ye wanna play it with me tonight, is it?"

After noisily sucking his fingers, he finally looked up from his plate to meet her gaze with apathy. "If ye want someone ta say somethin' to him, do it yerself. But don't pretend it's fer *him*."

"What's that supposed to mean?"

"All ye want is yer clear conscience, Seersha, and that's all ye're gonna get. 'Cause we both know Seamus doesn't listen ta anyone else's reason if it doesn't align with his. I'm willin' ta bet Halsey Ambrosius goes about carvin' her own path in much the same fashion. So if ye're lookin' fer a fight ye'll most certainly lose, by all means…" He gestured with one hand toward Seamus, Halsey, and Rafer, then shot Seersha a devious grin.

She folded her arms, stared back at him, and tapped her foot on the grass for a good five seconds before sighing and giving up. "Ye know, if ye spent less time crammin' everythin' inta yer gob, the rest of us might spend more time listenin' to the wisdom comin' out of it."

"Aye, but I'm famished."

"'Course ye are." Seersha shook her head and strode across the grass toward the big house. "I'm gettin' another drink. What d'ye fancy?"

"Surprise me."

CHAPTER TWELVE

Halsey was incredibly impressed by Seamus' ability to charm his uncle into giving up the cups and liquor bottle on his way to the picnic table. Having her beside him made it easy to start the conversation with a brief reintroduction, after which Rafer thought it perfectly reasonable that Seamus would want to bring the drinks over as an excuse to inform his parents that he'd come home. And that Halsey had returned to Ireland, of course. Neither of which any of the Havalons had expected tonight.

At least, she wanted to believe Seamus was incredibly charming or had enough sway with his family to take his requests seriously. There was always another option. That the Havalon Clan was willing to concede to whatever Halsey Ambrosius the Alpha Hunter might have wanted, whether or not they agreed with it. She'd earned the new title after a night of literal blood, sweat, and tears she hadn't let herself shed.

Just because the silverback alpha died with my axe in his

chest doesn't make me qualified to call the shots. Especially in another Clan. Seamus knows what he's doing. Follow his lead.

So she did.

After taking leave of Rafer, who didn't seem particularly fond of returning to the thick tension emanating from the picnic table, Seamus and Halsey headed across the yard toward them and didn't stop again along the way.

She felt a slew of Havalon eyes on them, though no one said a word and no one tried to keep them away. The majority of the family returned to their regular evening activities as if there hadn't been a strange and unorthodox *cruinniú* called in the center of it, with a strange and unorthodox visit from a Clan the Havalons hadn't hosted at their home in decades.

As Halsey wondered how they would insert themselves without interrupting and drawing all the attention to themselves, Seamus stopped a dozen feet from the picnic table and gently nudged her arm. When she halted, he pulled two plastic cups off the stack and handed them to her. "Here."

She felt ridiculous standing there with two empty cups, but he tucked the stack under one arm and expertly cracked the seal on the liquor bottle before pouring three fingers into each with a steady hand.

The semi-sweet, grainy smell of flavorful whiskey wafted from the cups like a punch to the face. A soft chuckle escaped her as she looked at Seamus before returning her focus to holding the small glasses steady. "Whoa. No ice or mixers or anything, huh?"

"All part of the *cruinniú* tradition," he murmured.

"So the more they drink, the more they'll be willing to let us sit in on the grownup discussion, huh?"

Seamus smirked. He finished pouring the second drink, then flipped the stack of cups from under his arm to fill the one on top as well. "Trust me, it has nothin' ta do with how much they drink."

"Then what are we doing?"

"Serving." He finished the final neat pour, then turned toward the table again. "Reckon ye can figure which ones are the guests tonight?"

"You mean besides me?"

He looked at her from the corner of his eye. "Ye can stop thinkin' 'bout yerself as a guest, Hal. Ye aren't. Ye earned yer place at that table the last time ye were here, and everyone knows it. Besides, if ye're gettin' yerself involved in this with me tonight, ye're showin' everyone ye're ready ta be a part o' this all the way. Havalons-only kinda thing."

The weight of his words settled into her awareness, but surprisingly, it wasn't a hard decision. The Havalon Clan had taken her in as if she'd always been one of their own. They'd believed every word of what she and Brigham had told them. That the Mother of Monsters had returned, monsters were changing everywhere, and they needed to take a stand and prepare themselves for what could potentially be another great war *right now*. They hadn't been suspicious of the Ambrosius cousins' arrival, they hadn't turned the young hunters away, and they hadn't held a grudge for their family's multiple slights against their Clan.

If she needed to commit herself to being part of the Clan in all regards, including participating in this strange meeting, she could do that. What all three elemental Clans faced now was so much bigger than any family alone. It involved them all, because they were the only ones left to stand against the coming danger.

After rolling her shoulders steadily back so she wouldn't spill the cups she held, Halsey drew a deep breath and nodded curtly. "Right. I can be a Havalon for a night, sure. No problem."

"Hopefully it sticks 'round a wee bit longer than a single night, but it's a fine start."

Halsey almost looked at him again but decided against it when the words popped wryly out of her mouth. "As long as no one's expecting me to change my name or anything."

She instantly felt like a moron for saying that out loud, especially given the nature of her and Seamus' developing but still undefined relationship.

Oh sure, Halsey. Let's make flippant references to name changes and marriage 'cause that's totally something on the table.

Seamus surprised her with a low chuckle, but neither one of them looked at the other. "Ye can keep yer name, Hal. At least for tonight."

She pressed her lips together and forced herself to stare at the table while actively *not* clenching the cups hard enough to make them jump from her fingers and spill all over the grass.

He only said that to screw with you. Don't let it get under your skin.

No, Halsey Ambrosius was not marrying anyone anytime soon. It was and had always been the last thing on her mind. But if she *did* go down that path someday, far in the future, she imagined joining another family wouldn't feel much different from the way she'd already joined the Havalon Clan.

First elemental to transmute sand into a copper ball that does all the heavy lifting for me. First elemental to suddenly sprout new magic nobody knows a damn thing about. Wouldn't be all that weird as the first elemental to get hitched to another elemental. I don't think that's ever happened before...

"Ye still haven't answered my question," Seamus added, ripping her from the strangest tangent of thought she'd had in a while.

Halsey brushed it aside and cleared her throat. "Can I find which two of these things are not like the others?" Now that they were so much closer to the table, she'd already inherently singled out the two Grendier Clan visitors. A man and a woman, neither of them much older than forty, with sharply aquiline features, bronzed skin, and blond hair in only slightly differing shades. With a snort, she added, "I'm sure I'll figure it out."

"Aye, I believe ye may." Trying to hide a smile, he nudged her arm with an elbow. "The first two go to our guests. I'll pour, and ye deliver. Aye?"

"I mean..." She didn't think she could look at him again without bursting out laughing. "They better be good tippers."

Then she headed toward the table. She focused on walking like a normal Havalon who was certain she was supposed to be here and wasn't concerned about being noticed, called out, and turned away from butting her nose in where it wasn't wanted.

Only after she'd made it halfway did she hear Seamus' next soft chuckle as her wry joke finally hit home.

See? Maybe it's easier to be a Havalon than you thought.

As she approached the table, the conversation didn't change. There was no way they hadn't noticed her presence, but no one removed their gaze from the Grendier woman currently speaking.

"...was empty when we arrived. Abandoned, perhaps, but we do not think it was in haste to get away. Nothing else seemed out of place."

Halsey chose the next momentary pause in the woman's words to lean carefully forward between the two Grendiers and set one cup in front of the woman, then the second in front of her male counterpart. Neither of them acknowledged her or the drinks, but the man continued the story where his partner had left off. His words carried the same tinge of a European accent she couldn't regionally pin down.

"Nor did we find any signs of living creatures having used the building as shelter. No remains of feeding. No waste production." He leaned slightly forward over the table and licked his lips before adding the detail that clearly bothered him the most. "There was not so much as a single bed. No blankets, pillows, rags, nothing. But we could not simply turn around and leave, so we dug some more..."

Not wanting to draw any more attention by standing there behind the newcomers and blatantly listening to everything they said, Halsey quickly removed herself. She power-walked back toward Seamus, who had poured two more drinks and was waiting for her to collect them.

"Hear anythin' good?" He smiled as he handed over the cups.

"An abandoned building and no signs of life." She shrugged and shook her head. "Doesn't sound weird to me."

"Ah, well. We'll get the gist of it soon enough. Those go to my folks next."

Nodding, Halsey made yet another trip to the table to deliver what was apparently the ceremonial drink required for all official Havalon gatherings. It was easy to spot Cillian and Fiona Havalon among the dozen people sitting at the table. However, the grimly set line of Cillian's lips within his dark, white-flecked beard and his deeply furrowed brow made a startling contrast to his usually jovial expression. His wife Fiona sat beside him, her back straight and her hands folded in her lap as she listened impassively to their guests' tale. Her expression gave nothing away.

As before, neither of Seamus' parents acknowledged Halsey's presence or the two small cups she set on the table in front of them.

"It was as if the things had hardly used their shelter," the Grendier woman added. "Yet there is to be no doubt it *was* their shelter. We tracked them there ourselves, which is what makes everything afterward that much more…concerning."

Halsey left the table again for one more round of "serve the drinks," though now her curiosity had been stoked enough to make her instantly recount a summary of what she'd heard to Seamus. They didn't discuss the information, which would have wasted time when he seemed so certain they would be welcomed at the table after the drinks were served. They could listen to the rest of the story from there.

So she walked quickly back and forth, setting drinks in front of two elementals at a time without disturbing the flow of the conversation or receiving the slightest acknowledgment from any of them. Seamus gave her clear instructions on whom to deliver drinks to next, making it clear there was a specific order to this process without explicitly saying it or explaining why.

Each time she reached the table, she got a tiny snippet of conversation that seemed wildly opposed to what she'd heard on the last trip.

"…don't just disappear like that…"

"…considered the fact that our minds and perhaps even visual perception were somehow affected…"

"…inconclusive results with very little physical evidence…"

Jesus, this sounds more like a meeting with Dr. Frankenstein. We don't do that kinda monster.

On her final return trip from the table, she stopped in front of Seamus with a sigh. "Okay, now what?"

"Take a cup." He handed her only one this time and nodded.

Halsey peered into the drink then glanced over her shoulder for a quick scan of the table again. "I'm pretty sure we already got everyone."

"Aye. That one's yers."

"Mine?" Her eyebrows shot up in surprise. "I'm actually more of a beer fan…"

"Well, it's not fer drinkin' *now*, so ye have a bit o' time still ta wrap yer head around the idea." Seamus dipped his head. "It's best if ye take the seat on the right. That way, my folks can see ye there without havin' ta shift 'round any. I'll take the left." He lifted his whiskey at her in a silent toast.

Halsey blinked. "Okay, but seriously. What happens next?"

"I just told ye."

"So we're playing make-believe now? Because there's literally zero room for *one* more person at that table, let alone both of us."

"Hm." Frowning, he gazed over her head and stuck out his bottom lip in consideration. "Are ye certain o' that?"

Knowing what she'd seen at that picnic table all six times she'd made the trip back and forth, she spun in aggravation to see it for herself. She prepared to offer some quippy remark about how none of this alleged "ritual" made any sense.

Then she had to swallow whatever she might have said back down, because Seamus wasn't yanking her chain.

An entire two feet of extra space had opened up on both benches at the ends closest to them. More than enough room for Halsey to slip in next to Cillian's first cousin Beecham on the right and Seamus to settle next to his great uncle Taggert. All without anyone else seated on the wooden benches having moved an inch.

Her mouth popped open, and she blinked furiously. "How..."

Seamus playfully clicked his tongue. "What's the matter, Hal? Never enjoyed the subtleties of a little magical invitation before?"

He didn't give her any time to respond before he took off toward the left-hand bench.

Halsey laughed and headed after him, mentally kicking herself for not having considered how any of this might have turned out.

So those who serve at the cruinniú *get a spot at the table. Makes sense. And my family would call it a useless distraction meant to unsettle the balance of a selected Council's homeostasis...or some other stupid excuse. But now we're in, so I guess this is it.*

Moving as quickly, quietly, and unassumingly as possible, she reached the end of the picnic table as Seamus slid into his seat and placed his tiny plastic cup on the worn wood in front of him.

Even when she took her place in the seat where there had previously been no room, no one else looked at her, including Seamus. He watched the Grendier team from across the table, his expression open with a willing curiosity and intense interest. As if he'd been sitting there from the beginning.

Not wanting to break any of the protocol no one had bothered to explain to her, Halsey set her own cup on the table and slid her hands into her jacket pockets. The copper orb's cool, slick surface had once again become a welcome relief from the uncertainty around her, even when it wasn't immediately her responsibility to figure it out.

She scanned the six Havalons across the table from her, all of whom she recognized by sight if not by name. No doubt they all knew she'd taken her seat among them. An extra few feet on two wooden benches didn't simply grow themselves. Yet apparently, the proper way to attend a *cruinniú* was to acknowledge only the individual currently speaking and no one else.

That was difficult to do from the edge of the bench on the same side as the Grendier elementals.

Instead of fidgeting and leaning enough to effectively focus her gaze on the newcomers, which would have made her the only person at the table to move a muscle, she stared at the rough grain of the tabletop stained with wear and time and the elements. She kept her hands in her pockets, letting the orb both comfort her and stabilize her attention. All she had to do now was listen.

CHAPTER THIRTEEN

"Neither of us could discern what we were dealing with this time," the Grendier woman continued. "Of course, we utilized all the resources available to us. Historical records. The oldest accounts of the creatures that have walked this Earth over the centuries. We even submitted what physical evidence we managed to collect to our partnering research facility, hoping to find the slightest bit of information that would enable us to pinpoint what these things are. And, of course, so we could better understand how to engage it in the future."

"There was nothing," the man added solemnly. "No records. No mentions or possible cryptic allusions to a creature such as this. Then the lab reports failed to identify even a small percentage of the sample components we submitted. We ran the tests a dozen times. This is..." He sighed heavily and scratched the side of his head, his hair shorn so short it was only a shimmering layer of blond covering his scalp. "Well, quite frankly, it is a disturbing reality. Our Clan elders knew of no such monster, nor could they locate evidence of its kind ever having existed."

"Which is a dangerous assumption to make." The woman gestured toward her counterpart, not necessarily blaming him for having given up hope but clearly indicating their opinions differed in this matter. "We know the Blood Matriarch's children have been…changing over the last several months. Mutating. Evolving. Some are simply *devolving* to the point where the militia protocols upon which our families have depended for centuries no longer apply.

"Though challenging at first, this is a relatively easy obstacle to overcome. I trust the Havalon Clan has also implemented various…adaptations to standard procedure when faced with unusual behavior and responses."

The silence around the picnic table was heavy with the weight of all shared experiences, punctuated by pockets of laughter and carefree shouts from the Havalons not at the table. The noise in no way diminished the silence of the *cruinniú*, nor had it previously drowned out a single word of what the Grendier elementals had shared so far.

Well, now I get how easy it is for everyone here to ignore everyone else. I'll have to ask Cillian how they managed a magically soundproof table in the middle of a field.

Apparently, there was no need for anyone on the Havalon Council to verbally express their agreement with the Grendier woman. They had already experienced the same thing, which the Grendiers clearly understood.

"My brother is of the mind that new creatures are springing up from the ether without rhyme or reason," the woman continued slowly, choosing each word with care.

"He believes those we have mentioned here tonight are simply one of many different species out there with which no elemental Clan in history has witnessed or had physical contact. I cannot say this is impossible. Many things we have believed impossible have proven themselves the opposite as of late. But I do not believe it is the most likely explanation.

"So far, we have encountered nothing else remotely similar to this unknown species. All other targets, though mutated in some form or fashion, have their roots in what we *do* understand. These new ones? They do not. However, it is not mere speculation based on what simply has not yet occurred that convinces me my brother's theory will not stand. New creatures manifesting themselves for the first time after we elementals have known of the supernatural and dealt with it every day for centuries…"

The woman paused, then continued. "I believe this would be a messy process. Trial and error on the creatures' part, of course. If they had no ancestral bloodline with which to acquaint themselves and learn their species' modes of survival, we would notice their existence immediately. Attacks on the human population would be far more widespread and frequent, for one. Then there is the fact that these creatures have not exhibited the usual evidence of living, breathing things striving to fulfill the basic physical needs of their corporeal forms."

Halsey closed her eyes, trying to work out exactly what the woman was saying.

Does she think they've been hunting monsters that don't exist? Or are we talking about ghosts and spirits now and opening up a whole new can of worms?

"There is no doubt these monsters possess physical form." Now the woman sounded as if she were merely thinking out loud, trying once more to put the pieces together but with an audience this time. "Yet that physical form was not simply granted to them through happenstance. We live in a world with magic and monsters, but that does not change the laws of *universal matter*. They had to have come from *somewhere* because *nowhere* is not an option. New forms do not arise from the nothingness as an *effect* when there has been no *cause*."

The man beside her cleared his throat. "To be perfectly clear, Alvara makes no attempt to convince any of you these creatures come to us from…other worlds, despite how her chosen argument might make it sound. More specifically, no, these are not aliens."

A hushed, polite communal chuckle moved around the table, but it faded quickly. At this point, there wasn't much to laugh about.

The Grendier woman clicked her tongue in irritation but forewent admonishing her brother in order to continue with her theory. Instead, she went with something much more gracious that still carried a hint of annoyance. "No, I do not believe they are extraterrestrial, just as I do not expect anyone else to take such an offhanded concept seriously. Thank you for making this clear, Dietrich.

"What I *do* believe is these creatures have been hiding from us elementals for centuries, biding their time until the perfect opportunity presented itself. I believe these unusual beasts have had the ability to…transcend beyond our physical plane and back again for as long as they have been in existence. From what we have personally witnessed, they are quite adept at it.

"Our main concern at the moment is that we cannot prepare ourselves against such creatures with nothing more than conjecture and agreement upon the most likely scenarios. What we *need* is to accurately classify this monster, pinpoint its abilities, strengths, and weaknesses, and arm ourselves with the knowledge required to dispose of them."

"The Grendier Clan records hold no such information," Dietrich added. "Nor did our more scientific inquiries into the nature and composition of the physical samples these creatures left behind. As such, we have exhausted all readily available Grendier resources with nothing to show for it. And so we come, humbly and without expectation or further motive, to ask the Havalon Clan for assistance."

His sister nodded and drew a heavy breath. "As I'm sure you can imagine, we had hoped your Clan would possess some knowledge or understanding of these beasts. I do wish to make it clear that we are not in search of hard evidence or incontrovertible proof. We already know these creatures exist. So even if what you have consists of nothing more than stories, mere figments of the imagination at first glance, we are incredibly interested in learning about those as well. Anything you can provide is far more than what we currently have."

Another silence followed the Grendiers' plea for information, and Halsey wondered if anyone would speak up. Though she hadn't been at the table for the first half of the conversation and didn't have all the facts like the rest of the Havalon Council, she didn't need those details to realize they'd found themselves in a pickle with this one. Nothing immediately popped into her head regarding old stories about any kind of monster that might have fit the description the Grendier elementals had given. Still, she only had half the information and a fraction of the experience.

Decades of monster-hunting experience sat around her at this table. If not a single one of these elementals had so much as a suggestion, it meant this was bad.

Very bad.

Finally, the contemplative silence was broken by someone other than the Grendier siblings. Halsey was surprised that it was Seamus' mother, Fiona.

"Dietrich, ye said ye tried ta analyze test samples of certain…material these creatures left behind."

The man dipped his head. His lips pressed tightly together in a solemn line. "Yes."

"And…apologies." Fiona briefly closed her eyes to organize her words. "I don't quite understand what ye mean by yer tests' inability ta identify the sample components."

Alvara drew a deep breath, held it as she met her brother's gaze, then released a long, heavy sigh. "Yes, this is confusing. How far does your knowledge of forensic testing and analysis extend?"

Fiona lifted her chin. Her confidence as a healer, scientist, mother, and wife to the head of the Havalon Clan Council swelled enough to confirm that the one magic-less human among them deserved a seat at this table. "Far enough ta understand the type o' summary ye might offer a colleague. Includin' the number o' different tests and specifically which ones."

The Grendier siblings shared another knowing look, then Alvara replied quite plainly, "All of them."

Another heavy silence circulated around the table. This time, it had less to do with the weight of the issues they all faced together and more with the baffling answer.

Fiona's lips popped open in uncertainty as she shot her husband a sidelong look. Cillian's only reply was to raise his eyebrows and let her handle it. So Seamus' dark-haired, petite mother with the same brilliant blue eyes she'd given her son blinked at the Grendier siblings before muttering, "Come again?"

"We ran every available forensic evidence test known to both civilian humankind and…well, *us*, of course." Alvara's blonde hair was pulled tightly back from her face in a severe bun that accentuated the sharp angles of her face. She reached up to tuck a strand behind her ear as if it hadn't already been harshly plastered against her head. "Each one of them produced inconclusive results, without fail. The only thing the analyses did provide was confirmation that the material was not carbon-based, as we had assumed it would be. Beyond that, the samples contained zero natural compounds known and recognized on this planet, organic or inorganic. In other words, each test revealed one hundred percent unidentified material."

"I see." Fiona studied the picnic table with a contemplative frown, her blue eyes whipping back and forth in thought before she remembered herself and looked at Alvara. "I appreciate the explanation. O' course, it *does* make what we're lookin' at here a wee more difficult ta fully grasp."

"Indeed it does."

"But it lends more logic 'n I expected to the idea of it bein' aliens," Scully piped in with a wry laugh. "No offense ta either of ye's, so please don't take it the wrong way. It's just…" Cillian's brother swept his gaze around the table, then shrugged. "No identifiable compounds in a…whatever it was the damn beastie left behind. Sounds like somethin' straight out of a science-fiction film, doesn't it?"

Fiona snorted and murmured without looking at him, "One could also argue that nearly everythin' *this* family does should be right up on the shelf somewhere with *Harry Potter*."

Another round of low, marginally amused chuckles circulated the crowded table, and the comments briefly drew the conversation to a sustained pause.

If there had been only regular humans sitting around this table, those without magic, who knew nothing of the supernatural world, talk of science-fiction movies and fantasy books would have been the end of the conversation. To normies, the things they didn't understand could be explained away by their rational mind's astounding capacity to make logical excuses for experiences they couldn't comprehend. That was how it had always been, and that was how it was supposed to be.

Yet everyone sitting around this table knew otherwise. The only exception was Fiona Havalon. She was one of those rare cases, much like Halsey's grandfather Percival, who'd married into an elemental family knowing what they were capable of and ready to do whatever she could to help the cause.

Halsey bit her lower lip and studied the edge of the table.

If magic's totally normal and acceptable because it's part of our everyday lives, who's to say these things aren't *aliens? Except for the fact that elementals and monsters have been fighting each other for over thirteen hundred years.* Some *of us would've figured out how to find ETs if they were running around our planet and trying to hide themselves. Wouldn't be all that different from hunting monsters, and that's literally all we do.*

It was the same thought on everyone else's mind, which was why nobody took the aliens theory seriously. Yet no one had any other suggestions, either. As Halsey started to wonder if the Havalons would let this empty silence continue way past sunset and through the night, Cillian spoke for the first time since she and Seamus had joined them.

"I have a feelin' we're far from callin' this *cruinniú* to a close yet," the large, heavily bearded man offered before nodding at their guests. "If there's anythin' else ye have, however small it might seem, I would hear more."

Everyone at the table watched Alvara and Dietrich in expectant silence. The Grendier siblings shared a knowing look, then he nodded for her to continue.

"There is one final element we would like to add to this discussion." Alvara swept her gaze across the slew of Havalon elementals, then retrieved a small black duffel bag she'd left sitting beneath her on the grass. "Of course, we expect no one to take us on our word alone. Even when our Clans have no such quarrels as to foster mistrust between us."

The duffel bag thumped on the table, and the woman unzipped it as she continued. "We brought what we could to show you what we are dealing with in this unidentified creature. If it does not spark any type of recognition, at least you may all see for yourselves what little we have to work with."

She stood slightly, upended the small bag, and dumped its contents onto the middle of the table.

CHAPTER FOURTEEN

For a moment, they all simply stared at the scattered pile of brownish-yellow fragments. Though Halsey hadn't been able to look at either of the Grendier representatives while they'd shared what was no doubt the most alarming part of their story, she had a perfectly clear view of the "sample material" they'd brought. And like everyone else sitting around her, she had no idea what it was supposed to be.

"Looks like glass," someone finally offered.

"Frosted glass, maybe, aye. Same kind we used ta find in Gran's kitchen back when she wouldn't let us touch the *fine* dishes."

A few of the Havalon Council members chuckled, no less subdued than the other times so far.

"How d'ye know the *monsters* left all this behind?" someone else asked. "And not, ye know...a gang o' squatters bringin' all their fun shiny objects into abandoned buildin's ta make it feel more like home?"

The man who'd spoken sat on the other side of the Grendiers, which meant Halsey had no idea who it was or what kind of looks he was drawing from the people on his side of the table. She did have a wide-open view of everyone on the other side.

Seamus closed his eyes and remained perfectly silent. Fiona glared in the general direction of the Havalon who'd spoken, her eyes narrowed into disapproving slits. Cillian kept his focus on Alvara and Dietrich, though it was impossible to tell if the Grendier siblings noticed him gauging their reactions or if they'd turned their attention to the man who'd spoken out of turn.

Not exactly the best way to question the validity of this stuff, Haley thought as she studied the shattered pieces of what did look like thick pieces of brownish-yellow frosted glass. *Whatever it is. Could be anything, honestly, but we're all trusting these two wouldn't waste anyone's time with a bunch of lies...*

Which probably had quite a bit to do with why the Grendiers had come to the Havalons instead of the Ambrosiuses.

"How do we *know*?" Dietrich repeated as he gestured toward the pile of amber-colored material. "Aside from the fact that if we were to test one of these pieces right now, we would come up with the exact same inconclusive results as all the other tests we have run to answer the same question?"

He received only silence in reply, but the corner of Cillian's mouth quirked in slight amusement at the man's ability to call out a Havalon Council member who wasn't adept at putting his thoughts into words. Then Seamus' father cleared his throat and added, "I'm sure ye understand the growin' need for skepticism these days, Dietrich.

Nothin' 'gainst the two of ye or yer word that all this is truly what ye say 'tis, o' course."

"Of course we understand," Alvara replied quickly before her brother had a chance to voice frustration over being questioned. "This is only a small sample pool of the material we found in *both* buildings we searched after tracking the monsters back to...well, to what we suspected was the source of it all. Perhaps a den or warren. It seemed more appropriate that they'd used abandoned buildings in the countryside where humans were less likely to walk in on them and their privacy."

"More appropriate in what fashion?" The question came from another of Seamus' aunts, Maelis, who sat immediately beside Halsey with her face turned toward the Grendier siblings so Halsey couldn't see a sliver of the woman's expression.

Alvara's disbelieving voice explained, "Because of their form."

Halsey could only gauge half the table at that point, but Seamus, his parents, and the other four Havalons sitting there with them looked at a loss.

With a sigh, Alvara turned toward her brother and muttered something in German so softly and quickly that, despite Halsey's training in languages, she couldn't pick out a word. The siblings bickered in whispered German for a moment longer, then abruptly stopped. Dietrich shook his head fervently and scowled at the forest behind the Havalon estate's enormous backyard while his sister's irritated frown burned through the side of his face.

The Grendier woman smoothed back the top of her head, where every hair was already pristinely laid in place, and offered an apologetic smile. "Please do forgive my brother's lack of forethought in this matter. We have discussed our findings countless times in the last several days, and it is hard to keep track of who has received all the relevant details and who has not. It would seem that exhausting all our resources in this investigation has also exhausted us personally."

"Aye. A thing like this tends ta have that effect on even the best of us." Cillian slowly shook his head and offered an understanding smile. "No need ta apologize fer any of it. Not at this table, and not ta us. If it slipped Dietrich's mind ta explain the full scope, we won't blame him. Though I am rather curious ta hear what form these beasts have taken that makes the rest o' this make sense. Speakin' o' the big picture, o' course."

Alvara shot her brother another perturbed glance, then replied tensely, "We have seen them in action out in the wilds, which made this harder to believe when we realized the creatures were responsible for the carnage they had left behind with the surrounding wildlife. Even harder when we watched them disappear into thin air without warning when they caught wind of us watching them.

"Like we have discussed, there have been few monsters in this world for the last several centuries who possessed the ability to, for lack of a better phrase…physically teleport themselves to undisclosed locations. I realize we should have begun with this most important and disturbing fact about the creatures."

The woman paused for another deep breath, but instead of looking around the table, her blue eyes settled on the scattered pile of brownish-yellow glass in the middle of the table. "From what little we have seen of them so far, they seem to prefer inhabiting a humanoid form."

"Humanoid?" another man asked. "Hell, half the beasts we go after are humanoid—"

"We understand what there is ta know 'bout what the lot of us have fought before, Harman," Cillian interrupted firmly, successfully mitigating the uprising of irritation and confusion that was sure to erupt if the Council didn't feel they were being offered sufficient information. The Grendiers seemed highly concerned, but so far, they hadn't offered concrete proof that this allegedly "new" monster they'd stumbled upon was any particular threat. Or worth coming out to the Havalon estate to ask for help in identifying.

"There's plenty of 'em out there," another woman added. "All of 'em easily defined as humanoid. Ogres. Trolls. The bloody vampires way up north. Hell, even the werewolves tearin' apart *our* country 'til naught but a few months back are *humanoid*. And aye, they leave behind plenty. Dead farmers. Eviscerated livestock."

"Sometimes a claw or two..."

Halsey couldn't see who'd offered that last comment. Yet when the Havalons she *could* see shared knowing glances with each other and tried to hide their smiles, it was perfectly clear they were all thinking about the alpha werewolf's claw Halsey had brought back to the big house buried in her thigh.

"So you mean to tell us your werewolves in Ireland have left behind items like this?" Dietrich gestured roughly toward the pile. "That my sister and I have traveled all this way to be made the butt of crude jokes because we do not already have the information we came here specifically to find?"

"Dietrich, mind your tongue," Alvara chided under her breath. "There is no need to take this so far with our hosts. They have been more than willing to hear our plight—"

"And willing in equal parts to laugh at us like children afraid of nursey stories."

"Make no mistake," Cillian cut in, his voice booming across the table like a shotgun. "Those nursey stories have always served a specific purpose. At least those told in families like ours."

The table fell silent again, and Halsey dared to look away from the increasingly tense *cruinniú* for a glimpse at the other Havalons still enjoying their evening despite its odd interruption. No one seemed to have noticed the enormous outburst from their Council head in a voice that could send birds fleeing from their roosts if he wanted.

Kinda expected my ears to start ringing after that, but okay.

Cillian's shouted correction had served its intended purpose, though. Halsey appreciated the way the head of the Havalon Clan could accomplish so much through such unexpected means. Stopping the arguments short before they got out of hand, partially admonishing the Council member who'd spoken out of turn, and effectively pacifying Dietrich's short-fused temper by assuring the Grendier man nothing the elemental families dealt with was considered nonsensical or mere fairytale.

Because that was what the elemental families were here to ensure. That the children who were laughed at for being afraid of fairytales and bedtime stories remained normal human children. That they would never face the hard reality of monsters running rampant through the night or magic scattered across the globe to defend against them.

Their jobs were to take every fantastical detail seriously, even if it seemed preposterous to consider.

Swallowing thickly, Halsey looked up at the enormous head of the Havalon Clan, who was busy scanning everyone's faces, making sure his point had come across. He didn't notice one small Ambrosius elemental at the end of the table staring at him in surprise and gratitude.

Cillian understands what most of my family might not ever get. The world is changing. Everything we thought we knew is falling apart, and all those bedtime stories might end up being what saves us.

All it took was for the Council head to make his position known, and the rest of the Clan would follow in his footsteps. Which was one more example of how much more cohesive the Havalons were as a militia and a *family* than Halsey's own flesh and blood. Her own father had participated in what was essentially a coup of old Ambrosius Council members before him. All so he and his siblings could get their own mother off the Council, banish Greta into the wilds of their enormous Texas property, and pretend for years that the woman wasn't the only one among them who'd retained any dignity when it came to preparing future generations to deal with the mistakes of those who'd come before them.

When it was all said and done, Halsey wondered if she would prefer to stay here in Ireland with the elementals who understood the importance of paying attention as much as she did. Now more than ever.

It was a tempting thought. She could be happy here.

The Havalons had already accepted her as one of their own. She was sitting at the table for an emergency *cruinniú*, for crying out loud. The potential to do more for the fate of *all* elementals was much greater with an entire clan behind her to help with whatever she needed.

A clan who wasn't so distracted by their immense efforts to keep all their secrets that they couldn't see how it only kept tearing their family apart.

As if their personal thoughts and goals had been aligned the entire time, Cillian continued the conversation almost exactly along the same lines as Halsey's thoughts. Only without specifically mentioning her or any of the information she'd brought to them months ago for which they *hadn't* turned her away.

"Every bit o' information is precious to us these days," he began, sweeping his gaze around the table one more time until he finally settled on the Grendier siblings. "No matter how small or seemingly insignificant they may be. Now, I understand the difficulty in repeatin' the same messages more times'n ye can count and findin' it troublesome ta keep yer head straight because of it.

"As I'm sure ye've figured by now, this Council ain't the only decidin' body for the Havalon Clan. We're not a regime, nor do we adhere ta more structure'n serves us on the day ta day. Normally, I'd let everyone else here at this table hash it out on their own ta get whatever information they think necessary, both ta prepare ourselves for any monstrous potentiality and ta feel like we can accurately give the two of ye and the Grendier Clan the aid ye've requested."

When he paused, the enormous Irishman frowned

deeply. Everyone else at the table remained perfectly silent, hanging on his every word.

Cillian continued. "Fer this particular situation, 'tis well within my own rights ta declare this *cruinniú* receive a temporary call of respectful silence so our guests may continue their tale uninterrupted and unoffended. Then, Alvara and Dietrich, I would ask ye put together the rest of what ye're tryin' ta tell us as and as succinctly as possible before we all move on ta drawin' our own conclusions 'n decidin' what ta do next."

Some of the other Havalons at the table bowed their heads. Others nodded or shot their neighbors a quick look with indecipherable meanings. Most of them, however, gazed openly at the Grendier siblings, having taken their Clan head's declaration to heart. They would wait for every speck of necessary information to be delivered by their guests before the *cruinniú* came to a close.

Halsey watched Seamus' parents, instantly pleased to see Fiona unfold her hands and subtly reach out to settle one on top of her husband's loosely closed fist. They didn't acknowledge each other beyond that, but their shared support, confidence, and admiration was undeniable.

Then she had to quickly look away because the sight made her think of her dad. And her mom, and the fact that things would have turned out so differently if Aiden Ambrosius had Gillian there with him to gently cover his hand with hers over the last twenty years.

Mom has nothing to do with this. Neither does Dad right now, Halsey. Focus on the here and now. That's the only way these people are going to reach any kind of decision on how to move forward.

After Cillian's announcement, Dietrich and Alvara dipped their heads together to whisper again in fast, barely discernible German. Their private deliberation took only a few more seconds, then Dietrich nodded at the Havalon Council head. "We are grateful for the hospitality and willingness of your family to offer us whatever we may need, even if that first begins with the two of us providing… necessary revelations."

Her brother looked between Seamus' parents but said no more.

"Because of this," the woman continued. "Dietrich and I have decided to diverge somewhat from the initial objective of our assignment when the Grendier Clan Council selected us to make contact with the Havalon Clan."

Cillian offered no verbal or visual response, but Fiona's eyes widened slightly. The other Council members maintained the expectant silence their Council head demanded of them, but now the mood around the table had changed again.

Holy shit. Looks like disobeying Council orders doesn't run rampant only in the Ambrosius Clan.

Halsey didn't even think about it when she flicked her gaze toward Seamus sitting directly across from her.

When she did, he was already staring at her, and it looked a hell of a lot like he had the same thought.

CHAPTER FIFTEEN

Alvara continued. "We were instructed to bring these samples to you, provide a generalized description of what we know of these creatures and what we do *not* know, and ask the Havalon Clan to provide any opinions, suggestions, or ideas for how to trace the lineage of these creatures. This, we have done."

Dietrich tapped the tabletop three times in quick succession with an index finger, then cleared his throat. "We were also instructed not to provide your Council with the full scope of intelligence the Grendier operatives have gathered over the last week. Our Council's reasoning was twofold. First, they did not want us to color your view of these new creatures and leave you grasping at straws, offering extraneous guidance based on what you may assume we would want to hear. The second reason for this was...*der mist.*"

The man grimaced. His sister fixed him with a much gentler gaze this time, which seemed to be the only way she knew how to comfort him without close physical contact.

After listening to them both talk to the Havalons and interact with each other, Halsey had a feeling physical contact wasn't one of the Grendier family's top methods of comforting each other. Though the siblings were clearly experiencing tension, Halsey focused on forcing herself not to smile.

Guess my knowledge of cursing in German came in handy eventually. He's pissed. And that means these people are finally getting serious about what they came here to say.

She felt Seamus watching her again, but she didn't dare look up at him for fear of bursting out laughing at what was the absolutely wrong moment.

Finally, Dietrich seemed to get ahold of himself and continue this unexpected confession. "Our Council's second reason for ordering this was that they did not wish the Havalon Clan to receive the full scope of our acquired knowledge and intelligence, only to use it of your own accord in any future attempts to combat these beasts. Without first alerting the Grendier Clan to your intentions and requesting a similar boon of us for whatever aid we may be able to provide in such endeavors."

He let the words hang over the table. It was impossible to tell whether the Havalon Council members were merely shocked to silence or if they were having difficulty understanding the full meaning.

Alvara clearly assumed it was the latter because she rolled her shoulders back and nodded in support of her brother's confession before offering more explanation. "The Grendier Council does not wish you to fight these monsters on your own because they are under the impression that the Havalon militia is undertrained and under-resourced for taking on an unidentified creature of such… frustrating mystery. Which is why they ordered us only to share with you the most—"

"Thank ye, Alvara," Fiona replied for the entire Council. "Nae need ta explain yerselves any further. We understand the implications."

The Grendier woman clamped her mouth shut and nodded.

Halsey couldn't have guessed what any potential dispute between the Havalon and the Grendier Clans might have been. She hadn't even known about the feud between the Havalons and her own family until meeting Seamus for the first time.

Now, though, it seemed these two representatives of the Grendier Clan were serving as the same type of intermediary between the two families as Halsey and Brigham had months ago. Only these particular envoys were fully aware of their own Council's intentions and had brought their decision to disobey direct orders with them.

A tense discomfort hung thick in the air, coming mostly from Dietrich and Alvara now that they couldn't put the worms back *into* the can they'd opened. Finally, Dietrich smacked his lips and sighed. "These are difficult facts to discuss openly with those our Council would have us deceive. We *are* truly here to ask for your Clan's aid in any way possible, but concerning the methods we have been ordered to use in collecting this information… Well, my sister and I do not agree."

"Please accept our apologies for having allowed these

orders to taint our interactions with you so far," his sister added. "We believe the Havalon Clan is more than equipped to provide investigative aid and even combat support, should it come to that. This is why my brother and I agree we must amend the misconception."

She paused again, offering anyone in the Havalon Clan an opportunity to speak their minds before they continued this strange conversation. But the Council members had all been directed to hold their tongues, and even Cillian looked like he had nothing more to say until their guests divulged the full breadth of their intel on this new monster.

Halsey bit her bottom lip and wondered how many other outbursts and truth bombs would hit this table before Cillian finally released them from the hold of the *cruinniú*.

Maybe the Grendiers and the Ambrosiuses aren't as different as I'd thought. Or wanted to believe. And here's the Havalon Clan in the middle, getting all the shit from both sides. They're the only ones who still know how to run things with actual integrity.

A burning curiosity to know everything about the Grendier Clan she wouldn't have found in the Ambrosius Clan Library or studied during her training filled her, but that had to wait for another time. In some ways, it felt like this conversation was taking forever. Yet as long as a few more fun surprises popped up, it wasn't boring anyone to sleep.

"Everything we have already informed you of these creatures' abilities is true," Alvara began again, this time with humility and a hint of trepidation. "We have never seen anything like them before. They were swift, ferocious, and nearly impossible to track after they activated their capacity to disappear. At first, we thought it more likely to attribute their visual disappearance to advanced camouflage or a form of natural cloaking techniques. Speed, agility, and a keen survival instinct can make any monster attempt to disappear, as we all know from personal experience."

That made Halsey instantly think of the most recent monsters on her completed-mission list. The chimera's swiftness of flight, the barghest's extraordinary ability to leap immense distances after sneaking through the brush, the grindylow swarm's hive-like behavior as they scrambled from that pond…

Before they disappeared the instant she realized they'd responded to both her and the copper orb's combined magic, and she'd ordered them to fuck off.

"Our summary of forensic tests was also the complete truth," Alvara added, forging on despite the lack of response from anyone else at the table. Even amid their silence, the Havalon Council clearly sat with rapt attention to every detail. "What you see before you on this table does not contain so much as a microscopic level of any organic or inorganic compound in known existence.

"I wish this were not the case, but unfortunately, it is so. We cannot analyze, duplicate, or manipulate the substance by any of the various methods the Grendier Clan is well-versed in executing in our pursuit of understanding these creatures the way we monster hunters understand all those who have come before.

"What we have not fully disclosed, however, is the

manner in which we discovered these creatures, how we managed to track them down, and what we found when we followed that trail to its only possible end."

Oh, good. Looks like Seamus and I get a full recap of everything we missed because someone else ordered these two to lie about half of it the first time.

Halsey would have become impatient if not for the full picture that was about to be revealed to all of them at once. To her surprise, none of the Havalons displayed any sign of growing annoyance with having to sit through so many do-overs. Either they trained their operatives to exhibit masterful poker faces during high-tension interactions, or intensely prolonged fortitude ran in the family.

Knowing Seamus, even as little as she did, Halsey assumed the latter.

When no one interrupted the siblings' retelling of their tale, Dietrich picked it up where his sister had left off. "Alvara and I were assigned a simple scouting mission out in Romania nearly a week ago. Our intelligence had picked up various reports of hunters and fishermen stumbling upon mangled wildlife in the woods. Fully grown elk torn open from nose to tail as if by a single strike. Carcasses of smaller animals like rabbits and foxes tossed around the wilderness and left to rot...*after* those same bodies had been broken and turned inside-out. Two bears in two different locations, hundreds of miles away from each other, turned up in territory where bears are rarely known to roam. Each of them lay in pieces, scattered within a one-mile radius. As if the things had been...*surgically dissected, bit by bit.*"

It was a lot to hear, and the mental images finally

brought out a comparatively significant response in the Havalon Council members. Almost half of them grimaced to varying degrees. Some clicked their tongues and shook their heads. Cillian sighed, his lips tightly pressed together as his frown returned. Fiona closed her eyes and swallowed.

Halsey and Seamus shared another look, though she couldn't ignore the fact that it was nothing like sharing one with Brigham. The Ambrosius cousins could practically read each other's minds with glances. Trying to replicate that with Seamus came close, but she was distracted by wondering exactly what he was thinking. Whether or not it was a response to what they'd heard or merely his curiosity about how *she* was handling it. She promised herself she'd stop and focus on the issue at hand.

None of the elementals were strangers to gory scenes and bloody discoveries. That was part of the job, and if a monster hunter couldn't stomach it, they generally didn't become a monster hunter. But what had happened to these wild animals was a rare occurrence.

Under normal monster-hunting circumstances, it would have signified a dangerous monster getting sick, losing its mind, or growing too old to know its place. Yet none of those left behind the kind of grisly evidence currently being described.

"Naturally, we anticipated these reports leading us to some O-class beast on its last legs," Dietrich continued.

"The old and infirm ones," his sister clarified after noticing several confused frowns at the Grendier Clan's personal coding system.

He nodded without skipping a beat. "Of course, this is

not what we found. It took us nearly a full day to find the first creature we had not known we were hunting. By nothing more than pure luck, we finally stumble upon it in the midst of what we can only assume was its mode of feeding. We cataloged all the regular signs. The sounds, the scents, the severe quiet around the creature and its prey while it devoured its latest meal—"

"It did not devour that doe," Alvara cut in with a sharp glance at her brother.

"Did I not just explain the *regular signs?*"

The blonde woman turned toward the rest of the table. Her stoic self-control had cracked into a grimace of disgust as she recounted what had happened. "The monster had caught a young doe. But it did not consume the animal's flesh, as one would expect of any predator. At first, this is what it seemed to be doing, but there was no blood. No exposed flesh. No torn hide. Then we realized even with its neck pinned between the creature's jaws, the doe still lived. Even then, we waited for the monster to finish its meal, as full satiety does tend to significantly slow a target in pursuit. We were wrong about this as well."

Dietrich scratched his shorn head. "That thing did not eat. It hardly stirred. For four hours, we surveilled the area of the woods where it had caught its prey, but feasting did not seem to be the creature's intention. When the doe neither died nor ceased its screaming, we knew we could waste no more time waiting for the perfect moment, and we engaged. The thing was—"

He stopped short, glanced at the small cup of neat whiskey in front of him, then seemed to realize the drink was off-limits because no one else had touched theirs. "It was unnatural. Even for the type of creatures our Clans have been sworn to defeat since before the great war. It acted as if it had known we were there the entire time, and it fought back like nothing else we've encountered. The sheer *size* of it. And when we fully realized its humanoid form, instead of a more beastly shape that would have made its actions like those of any other supernatural creature, I could not—"

Dietrich lost his ability to continue, so his sister took over for him. "We gained only a single positive hit between the two of us before the creature disappeared. One moment it was there, fully engaged. Then it simply was not. I believe it acted on survival after one of our weapons struck its...shoulder, if we are to use humanoid anatomy.

"The sound it made could only be classified as a scream, though I have never heard its like. There was a flash of dark light, and the creature was simply gone. Infrared scanners showed nothing. There were no magical traces left behind as far as either of our elemental abilities could detect. Nothing we recognized or could use to hunt it down.

"Needless to say, the doe did not survive. It would not have anyway, but we were able to put it out of its misery. Not from any bite marks or the slash of claws or even broken bones, as far as either of us could see. The poor thing had been chased down, caught, made to think its life had ended, then simply...transformed. Changed." Alvara wrinkled her nose and shook her head. "These are not quite the words to describe—"

"Plagued," her brother muttered solemnly. "Afflicted. Tainted, yes?"

The blonde woman considered his suggestions for a moment, then dipped her head. "Just so. We did, of course, return the doe carcass to one of our Clan's research facilities in order to further study what had happened to it, but those tests provided inconclusive results. Our first of many.

"We have not since recovered any additional wildlife corpses contaminated with the same affliction, which leads us to believe that either the doe was an accidental target or the things have learned to clean up after themselves. Neither of these is beyond the realm of possibility, but we do believe the latter is more likely. The theory of their growing intelligence has also proven more supported by the evidence we *did* later collect during our continued pursuit of this…thing."

Another ensuing silence stretched for so long, the thought of hearing anyone else's voice nearly made Halsey's stomach turn.

They're right. The monsters we know don't do that. Whatever that is supposed to be. So this is either a monster we know that's now totally unrecognizable or something we've never seen before. Something that apparently only makes a mistake once in front of a monster-hunter team before changing its behavior entirely to avoid a repeat match…

Though no one at the table physically moved, a collective jolt of being jerked back to their shared reality rippled through the elementals when Liam grunted to clear his throat. "Ye did say ye couldn't find a trace o' the thing after it disappeared in the woods, aye?"

Both Grendiers nodded slowly.

Cillian's first cousin sitting on the other side of Fiona

folded his arms, then unfolded them again to spread them as wide as possible on the crowded picnic bench in all his confounded disbelief. "Then how in the world did ye manage ta find the damn thing again fer collectin' all this so-called evidence?"

The question had been on everyone else's mind in one form or another. While Liam had technically acted against Cillian's indirect order not to say a thing until the meeting was over, the Clan head looked fairly relieved to have his own kin asking the question instead of himself.

Alvara gestured with a flick of her fingers toward the pile of amber-colored glass in the center of the table. "When I shot the beast, the blast tore away a chunk of this substance you see in the samples here in front of you."

"Tore off how?" Fiona asked.

"This is what we cannot understand ourselves," Dietrich replied. "The possibility of it and the mechanics, you understand. Not that it happened."

Cillian's mustache bristled as he tightened the line of his lips. "Not a single elemental at this table harbors any doubt o' that, my friend. Ye've come ta us in good faith 'n then some. Don't let a wee bit o' discomfort keep ye from finishin' what ye started, aye?"

The blonde stared back at the Clan leader in mute shock, then dipped his head in acknowledgment and gratitude. Clearly, Dietrich Grendier wasn't used to receiving permission to speak his mind without being judged for it.

Halsey knew the feeling all too well.

"We did not discover the first sample merely by searching for the monster's trail," the man continued with a slightly renewed confidence. "Alvara speaks the truth of it. Her well-placed shot struck a shard of this substance off the monster's body before it disappeared. Seconds before it screamed…"

"We believe it reasonable to assume the flash of dark light came from within the monster itself," Alvara continued, now sounding exhausted and ready to be done with this conversation. "From beneath this hardened substance. We discovered no traces of blood or other possible bodily fluids to prove the thing was injured. Simply this hardened amber, for lack of better nomenclature. The material coated the entirety of the monster's exterior. Something like an exoskeleton, but of course quite a bit more durable and of an unidentifiable nature."

"More like living armor," her brother added. "This is currently our strongest theory."

"It is also likely that what composes this substance holds a double purpose. Or at the least, yields the same effect from two different processes. The hardened shell of its armor, yes. But these shards seem to be left behind no matter the nature of our interaction with this species. Like a snake shedding its skin."

Dietrich snorted. "If that snake bled from an injury and its blood also happened to *become* more skin the second it left the reptile's body."

"Hmm." The blonde woman didn't seem to appreciate that analogy, but lacking anything better, she had to concede that it got the point across. "In the crudest possible way, yes. Perhaps that is the closest illustration to the truth of it. Worn to protect them, shed by natural causes for however long the creatures wear this armor, and spilled in place of recognizable bodily fluids. These samples were collected from various sites where the monsters were sighted or injured. Not mortally, of course.

"As of yet, there seems no definitive way to kill the creatures. For the most part, the material we have collected was scavenged after the creatures had already taken their leave of the vicinity. A few from out in the open. Most of them from what seems to have been our discovery of one of their nests. Or dens. Perhaps there is a better word for this in English?"

"Ye've painted a clear picture already," Fiona replied. "And the abandoned buildings you mentioned?"

"They *were* abandoned when we found them," Dietrich grumbled. "Filled with this excess material we cannot identify nor understand. The monsters left behind no other trace of their existence there, but I am sorry. This is a detail we were ordered to manipulate—"

"There *were* no buildings," Alvara finished, looking the Council head's wife directly in the eyes. "The structures were made half of stone and half of this…living armor. We can only assume the monsters built these structures on their own and left to construct new ones after they sensed our approach. So many days spent tracking them down, and we somehow spooked them all off several hours before we arrived. Most likely before that."

"Can ye estimate a count of their numbers?" someone else asked.

"Not currently, no." Alvara shook her head. "Dietrich and I have only seen the one in person. The rest of our operatives who have attempted to capture one have no better estimation than we do. Our best guess is likely a dozen, judging by the amount of material collected and produced to erect the structures they had used for shelter.

"Catching one of these creatures has proven impossible. We cannot do it on our own, and our Council was hoping for any information that would make it possible for our operatives to acquire one of the beasts for further study before moving in to eradicate them. If nothing else, we are certain more than one of these things are out there and that they mean us harm.

"A number of our operatives have been gravely injured in their attempts to retrieve what my brother and I could not. Yet without knowing anything more about them, without so much as a clue as to their origins or a semblance of their etiology or what they might be capable of now and in the future, the Grendier Clan does not possess the necessary resources to accomplish our aim. Beyond that…"

Her brother released a massive sigh and looked at Cillian with pleading eyes. "This is far more than what we were ordered to divulge. And it is *everything* we know. Truly."

"Aye." Cillian dipped his head and stroked his beard as he contemplated what had been said. Then, for the first time since the conversation began to unravel, he offered the siblings a genuine smile that made his green eyes light up the way Halsey remembered from her first visit here. "Well, I'd say it's as good a start as any."

CHAPTER SIXTEEN

The casual, joking way Cillian had delivered that last line did wonders for the general mood around the picnic table.

Smiles broke out all around. Some of the Council members chuckled, and those who sighed instead did so in relief and an equal measure of amusement.

Even Fiona cracked a smile, which seemed fairly unusual on the woman unless one had also seen the more compassionate, empathetic, and easygoing side of her. Halsey hoped they all might get to that point soon. With untouched cups of poured whiskey sitting in front of them and the last hour taken by the Grendiers' story, she imagined they had a *long* way to go if they wanted to catch up with the pervasive air of geniality and celebration filling the Havalon property.

At first, it seemed as if Alvara and Dietrich didn't quite know how to react to Cillian's levity. When no other jokes, suggestions, questions, or ideas were immediately forthcoming, the blond man chuckled wryly and asked, "Are we to take this Council's silence as a continued lack of suggested aid for our Clan despite our earlier confession or merely mute shock?"

Cillian's next laugh almost sounded like the rolling, thunderous boom of laughter she remembered so fondly from her last visit. It didn't even matter that the night of merrymaking had been interrupted by a werewolf fight. The sound of his amusement made her smile as she remained silent on the far end of the picnic bench. It felt like everything was balancing on the precipice of returning to normal again.

Or as normal as possible after the mind-bending revelations the Grendier siblings had shared with the *cruinniú*.

"A bit o' both, admittedly," the Clan leader replied. "I speak only fer meself when I say that, while far more illuminatin' than the content of yer original tale with all its half-truths, hearin' the fullness of what ye know 'bout these creatures still doesn't fan the flames o' recognition. Honestly, I can't even say 'tis more like a spark or the low glow of embers. But if any other o' my kin here have anythin' comes ta mind they feel like sharin', now would be the time."

It was a clear invitation from their leader that the time for holding their tongues was over. Halsey expected a wide range of questions to fill the air over the table, but there was only silence.

While Cillian waited slightly longer in case anyone else happened to come up with something their Clan leader had not, the other Council members shared looks with their neighbors or finally looked beyond the confines of the magically soundproofed table. The other goings-on around the property represented a much-needed reprieve from the discussion that had already taken so much of their evening.

After it was clear no one intended to speak up and offer suggestions or ideas they clearly didn't possess, Cillian sighed and dipped his head toward their guests. He held the Grendiers' gazes in a manner that silently imbued his words with more authenticity and genuineness than any other reaction could have managed.

"From one elemental to another, I wanna thank the two of ye fer trustin' this Council's *cruinniú* enough ta act against yer trainin' 'n follow yer guts anyhow. That's a damn hard thing ta do, and we owe ye our gratitude fer elevatin' the truth. Even if it ends up bringin' ye both down on the totem pole of yer own militia."

The siblings didn't say anything, but their curt nods and barely perceptible smiles made it clear they were proud of their decision to reveal the full truth. Plus, more than grateful to be acknowledged for such.

Cillian continued with another small frown darkening his features, though the lighter air of finality and the relief that came with it colored everything he said. "If I could drum up anythin' I reckoned might help ye, I'd do so in an instant. An old tale or proverb, some strange mention in any of our records, a meanin'less warnin' from the past... Hell, even a *memory* of a warnin' would be more than I can offer in terms of identifyin' this hellish thing showin' itself on yer lands and kickin' up such a mighty storm for the Grendier Clan.

"Believe me when I say there's nothin' I'd love more than ta be able ta give ye *somethin'*. Aye, I realize this ain't exactly what ye were hopin' ta hear from us after comin' all the way out, but the Havalon Clan thanks ye for yer honesty 'n trust. We welcome ye here in our home with open arms fer as long as ye feel like stayin'. And, o' course, if there's anythin' else we can provide to lighten even a wee bit o' the burden ye're carryin', ye only have ta ask."

"Thank you," Alvara replied softly. "All of you." She looked at her brother, who raised an eyebrow and nodded, which was apparently the only response she needed before continuing. "Since it has been offered, we would also request a moment more of your Clan's time to join us for a…lightning strike of the mind together."

The two blond elementals looked back and forth across the faces staring back at them, open and graciously eager to receive everything the Havalons were willing to offer.

No matter how well they'd all held their composure during the discussion, the Havalons found it nearly impossible to hide their amusement at the Grendier siblings' fault of translation. Someone snorted. Another elemental sniggered before choking it off with a bowed head. From Halsey's side of the table came a bark of laughter followed by a harsh smack. Whether it was from the man who'd laughed or one of his neighbors, she couldn't tell.

Then Fiona broke into a wide, gloriously beaming grin, an exact replica of which she'd passed on to her son, and pointed at her own head. "I reckon ye may've meant *brainstormin'*, if ye don't mind me sayin' so."

"Ah. Brainstorming." Alvara snapped her fingers in recognition. "Yes, this is it." She turned toward her brother and let off a violent string of criticism in another language.

Halsey expected to hear German again. When she

didn't, it took her a moment to realize the siblings were arguing in fluent Russian.

Damn. Looks like Grendier monster-hunter training might even be more hardcore than mine was. Takes a lot to argue with your relative in even two different languages, and I bet they could pull it off in three.

When the Grendiers' fierce but short-lived, whispered spat ended, Dietrich whipped his head away from his sister and nodded at Cillian and Fiona. "Yes. Brainstorming. Our Clan has always been scientifically minded, intent on cataloging facts and forming viable theories before acting on any number of practical likelihoods. It has served us well, but at this point, we believe the rigidity of the process is unwavering in the extreme. Likely even to a fault. We would very much appreciate this brainstorming with your Council for any applicable hypotheses we may be allowed to bring home with us when we return. Provided, of course, the Council head allows it."

"Ye wanna pick *our* brains, eh?" Cillian barked another laugh and slapped a hand on the table. "Well, I can't say how much good it'll do ye, but aye. Ye're welcome to it."

The rest of the Havalons broke into small smiles and chuckles at that, but the Grendier siblings remained all business until they were satisfied with their attempts to glean anything of use from their fellow elementals.

"Now, we are most interested in finding possible alternatives to where these beasts could have originated. How, why, or even potential explanations for their astonishingly evolved capabilities. Not only with their physical makeup and survival mechanisms but in their ability to learn and make vast improvements in their individual and group thought patterns to…"

"To thwart us every time we devise a new strategy against them and attempt to implement it," Alvara finished for him.

He shot her a curt look of surprise, then nodded before tossing a hand to accentuate his casual dismissal of what had already been discussed. "Excluding the unlikely and fallible possibility of these creatures having made their way here from beyond the cosmos, we have conceived only two other scenarios that hold even a small measure of weight.

"The first, as my sister has told you, was my suggestion that with all the other changes in monsters and the supernatural over the last several months, we may now be looking at a situation where new monsters are manifesting themselves without pedigree but with full awareness of their own instincts and capabilities. Alvara will tell you this is a preposterous ideology to hold in any high regard."

"I *have* told them," his sister muttered to another round of free-flowing chuckles from the Havalons.

"Ah, yes. You did." The man released a small laugh before continuing. "The second possibility, my sister's favorite, is that this particular species, if not a number of others we have yet to discover, has experienced an extreme and law-defying evolutionary jump. That their 'ancestors,' which must naturally be the previous generation, have been so affected by the odd changes that they became entirely new versions of much more recognizable and manageable predecessors. To change with the times and create new methods of survival to last them far beyond the day these changes cease to surprise us.

"We would like to ask all of you, now that you have every piece of information in our possession, if any other potentialities come to mind. We are more than happy to test any theory, no matter how absurd it may seem. If anything strikes you as even slightly important, now is the time to express those thoughts."

The table fell silent, each elemental racking their own brains for the tiniest sliver of possibility that hadn't been mentioned.

Halsey expected one or two of them to speak up and voice their ideas, but it seemed the Grendier siblings had expressed the only viable options anyone could conceive of. The Havalons were out of ideas.

However, Halsey had been mulling over the possibilities since she'd first realized the guests were here to discuss their cluelessness about a certain monster. Beyond the three semi-likely scenarios that had already been voiced, she wondered how these new monsters might fit into the scheme of what she and Brigham had discovered over the last several months.

There weren't any *new* monsters, as far as she could tell. With all the reports coming in of most monsters not acting the way they always had, all three elemental Clans were well aware of what was happening in the world, if not precisely how or why. Those changes had made themselves apparent shortly after the Ambrosius cousins had discovered the empty silver coffin. The Mother of Monsters hadn't wasted any time affecting her creatures in ways her arch-enemies couldn't predict.

If the Blood Matriarch had returned to create *new* monsters in addition to the ones she'd left behind before being sealed beneath the sea for a thousand years, the elementals would have noticed before the Grendiers discovered these new creatures that armed themselves and built their own shelter structures.

Just because a thing hasn't been discovered yet doesn't mean it hasn't existed until then. Like the silverback alpha. Werewolves can't talk, but Rolfr Magnusson did. I bet that wasn't new, either. He simply hadn't let an elemental see it until he was ready to commit suicide by monster hunter.

She swallowed thickly, trying to piece all the puzzles together in her mind so she didn't end up sounding like a complete idiot when those sitting with her inevitably questioned her suggestion from every possible angle.

The silence of the *cruinniú* continued, then Cillian clapped his hands together and nodded. "Well, then. It seems ye've tasked us with somethin' might need a wee bit longer ta finish than a few minutes at the table. The two o' ye're more'n welcome ta stay here with us for however long ye like, and if any o' my Clan has a sudden realization 'bout—"

"They could be left over from *before* the great war," Halsey blurted.

For the first time since she'd shown up at the estate, every Havalon finally turned to look at her. None of them seemed surprised to see her there. Of course, they must have known she and Seamus had joined them despite not acknowledging it.

Yet the surprise was still in their expressions.

Shit. Was I not supposed to say anything?

Halsey looked urgently at Seamus.

The hint of a smile graced his lips, and he raised an eyebrow in amusement.

"That's an interestin' thought, Halsey," Cillian slowly replied. "Feel free ta speak the rest o' yer mind."

She tried not to grimace. Her first instinct was to profusely apologize. For interrupting him, for sitting in on the Havalon Clan's ritual meeting, for drawing attention to herself yet again with the kind of ridiculous theories her own family would have suspended her for voicing.

But she didn't have the chance.

"Yes." Dietrich leaned forward for the first time to gaze down the line of people sitting between him and the young elemental who'd spoken up. "A provoking concept indeed. I am interested in hearing how you came to such an unexpected conclusion."

Halsey had no idea whether Cillian's comment about speaking her mind was genuine or if it was another dismissal like she was used to getting from her Clan, albeit much more polite. Not knowing what to do next, she looked at the Havalon Clan leader with wide eyes and waited for him to nudge her in one direction or the other.

"By all means, lass." He gestured toward her with a growing smile. "Illuminate us, if ye would."

She'd grown up experienced in being the center of attention within the Ambrosius Clan. Both as her family's best monster hunter and occasionally as Aiden's daughter, who tended to get herself into more trouble than she could get herself out of on her own. More recently, it had been the latter.

Yet being the center of the Havalon Council's attention, surrounded by all these people she truly respected, and being taken seriously as someone with a valuable opinion that *mattered*… That was different.

She froze, feeling more out of place than ever before in her life because she realized how much she didn't belong here. She didn't belong anywhere when she thought about it. Now she was only digging a deeper hole for herself by trying to think she could be part of this and not screw it up.

A gentle pressure settled on the toe of her boot, and she looked at Seamus again.

He still smiled at her, though now some other form of message entered his expression. She felt like she was supposed to understand. When his blue eyes flicked toward the small plastic cup of whiskey in front of her, his words of encouragement before they'd started delivering drinks returned to her.

"Ye earned yer place at that table the last time ye were here, and everyone knows it. Besides, if ye're gettin' yerself involved in this with me tonight, ye're showin' everyone ye're ready ta be part o' this all the way. Havalons-only kinda thing."

And she understood.

Offering Seamus a tiny smile and what she hoped wasn't too conspicuous a nod, Halsey turned back, inhaled, and opened her mouth to why she genuinely believed she'd landed on the truth.

CHAPTER SEVENTEEN

"Just because something was recently discovered doesn't mean it didn't exist before its discovery," Halsey began, slowly moving her gaze from one attentive face to the next without focusing on any. She felt absurd for stating her own thoughts out loud to start off the explanation of her "provoking concept." Then again, no one else here could read minds, so they were all hearing it for the first time. "Take literally every other discovery on the planet, right? Hell, Pluto was only discovered in 953, but obviously, it's always been there."

"We understand the concept, miss," Alvara cut in, leaning farther forward than her brother so she could see the young elemental's face. "But I do not believe celestial bodies are relevant to our current situation."

"No, they're not. It was only an example. But everybody gets the point, right? I'm thinking maybe, with all these changes we've been seeing over the last few months, these creatures you found finally felt like it was the right time to come out of hiding. It explains why none of us have seen them before. It explains how they've managed to stay hidden from elementals for centuries, how they were able to pivot so quickly when they realized they'd been discovered by Grendier hunters…"

She gestured toward the siblings, hoping to get the point across that she gave them full credit for all the new information and for sharing it with those gathered at this table. "You even talked about how quickly they seemed to learn and develop. Being able to disappear. Thwarting your attempts to injure them with more than a single shot or capture one so your Clan can figure out what they are. Building structures, strategizing to stay one step ahead of you. Honestly, after everything you told us, it feels more like these things have already had plenty of experience with elementals. Maybe even for thousands of years—"

"Now I have ta stop ye right there, Halsey," Liam interrupted from the other side of the table beside Fiona. "If I may?"

Trying not to look too upset about being given leave to speak and systematically interrupted—which *did* feel like her experiences in meetings with her Clan Council— Halsey nodded and gestured toward him.

"Many thanks." Liam dipped his head, then spread his hands and lightly chopped them on the table as he formulated his words. "Now, I can't say this theory of yers doesn't make any sense a'tall. Honestly, it caught *my* attention 'n made me think. Every wee bit of it makes a hell of a lotta sense. Except for the idea o' these things comin' from *before* the great war and the Ice Age, where everyone and everythin' but *our* ancestors got wiped out in the process."

"Aye, that's a bit of a major obstacle," Moya added

beside him. Halsey didn't know if the woman was one of Cillian's sisters or cousins, but it was hard not to recognize the pile of dark curls haphazardly spilling from the top of her head and her full, perpetually ruddy cheeks. *"Nothin' survived the great war other'n the Clans, who scattered 'cross the globe ta keep up the good fight. 'Tis an admirable attempt at a solution, lass, but it's also the easiest ta poke holes in."*

"Even so," someone else added conversationally. "The idea that these monsters've always been here is an intriguin' one. Might be the things've been hidin' in the dark all this time, waitin' for a future where the whole lot of us're so preoccupied with figurin' out the others..."

"...maybe one of the first..."

"...intelligence and speed, plus their other abilities. Kinda makes ye think o' the alphas, don't it? Every monster kind has one o' them..."

"...not *that* different from all the others..."

It seemed everybody was suddenly talking at once. Halsey bit her lower lip.

They're getting this totally wrong. All because I thought it would be a great idea to keep the most important facts about monsters and alphas and what actually *survived the great war to myself.*

Brigham also knew about the Blood Matriarch having been released from her prison when the crew of a Viking longship had managed to pull it aboard. Rolfr Magnusson had been one of those Vikings. Halsey was sure of it. Which meant the alpha monsters of this world, created *after* the great war and the "fresh start" every elemental believed their kind and humanity had received, had also been on that Viking ship. With the same man who'd become the silverback werewolf alpha and had begged Halsey Ambrosius to release him.

If these new monsters the Grendier siblings had "discovered" were alphas from that Viking ship, the elementals since then would have discovered the species long before now. Just like they'd discovered, cataloged, studied, and learned to hunt, fight, and defeat every other monster in existence.

The humanoid things that blighted their wildlife prey, bled chunks of their own living armor, and built living structures out of themselves were *not* alphas from that ship. They were something else entirely.

Now the arguments around the table were going nowhere fast because none of these people knew the truth of their history. Halsey's own Clan didn't even want to *face* the truth. They'd done unspeakable things in the last twenty years to keep pretending they hadn't heard the facts so they wouldn't be forced to drum up enough courage to face them.

The voices built around her, Havalons and Grendiers alike, calling out various opinions on how they could take what Halsey knew and twist it to fit their own known shape of the world without having all the facts.

I have to tell them. I have to. It changes everything.

Peeling her gaze off the tabletop, she looked up and tried to meet someone's gaze. No one was looking at her. So she had to insert herself into the chaotic conversation somehow, which seemed impossible when no one was paying attention to the single Ambrosius elemental.

"That's not actually true." She slightly raised her voice in the hopes that someone would notice. It didn't work.

"Excuse me," she tried again, raising her hand in case a bit of movement did what her voice couldn't. "You guys are looking at this the wrong way…"

"…then there *must* be something in our records *somewhere*!" Dietrich shouted while banging a fist on the table. "Yet nothing whatsoever exists. Unless someone here has not been entirely forthcoming about the knowledge held by their own Clan—"

"Now, wait here a minute." One of the Havalons pointed an accusing finger at the blond man. "Do ye truly dare ta name *us* a Clan of liars when ye told us yerselves ye'd been sent ta do just that ta us?"

"My brother has not called anyone anything. He merely wishes to—"

"Aye, well, he might *merely wish* ta step off our land if he can't keep from pointin' the finger at everyone but himself."

"And if he did, Neil, 'tisn't yer call ta make."

Halsey drew a deep breath and let it out in a long, slow sigh, glancing from one angry face to the next. Of course tensions were running high. For the first time, the only three elemental families in existence for the last several hundred years had no idea what they were facing or how to deal with it. In essence, the world's most powerful protectors had found themselves without knowledge, without effective arms against the new threats in their midst, and all but powerless.

Now they're gonna tear each other apart because that's easier than everyone admitting they made mistakes and don't know everything about everything.

Pressing her lips together in a grim line, Halsey scanned the faces down both sides of the table one more time, then sat up straight and looked for Seamus.

Fortunately, he hadn't gotten up and left, which part of her had expected him to do. She was on the verge of doing the same herself. He was already watching her with so much disappointment and hopelessness that his gaze felt like a plea and an apology wrapped up into one.

He doesn't know how to handle this either. Because he doesn't know what I do.

Seamus clearly wouldn't stand up in front of his entire family and tell them to knock it off so Halsey could speak. She wouldn't have expected him to. If their positions had been reversed, she probably would have sat there patiently like he did, waiting for the older generation of elementals who were supposed to be smarter, stronger, and more capable to get their shit together and quit acting like children.

Okay, fine. Time to take a stand again, Hal. Let's go.

After taking another few seconds to steel herself, Halsey sighed. In one swift movement, she pushed herself up off the picnic bench, stepped aside to stand in the grass at the head of the table, and shouted, "This isn't helping anybody! Can we get back to the actual discussion part? Because I really—"

Damn it.

There was no point in continuing her thought because the first part of it hadn't been received anyway.

Fiona was the only one among them to catch the single

voice shouting, and her eyes widened when she saw Halsey standing at the end of the table. The woman reached for her husband and tapped Cillian's forearm to get his attention, but the Clan leader was caught up in what someone else was saying directly in front of him, and he remained oblivious. Then Fiona looked around the table again at the elementals arguing with each other about conjecture and hypotheticals, and something like fear crossed her features.

It was an expression Halsey had never expected to see on the fearless human woman who'd married into a magical family of monster hunters and taken the whole thing in stride. But what could Fiona do if her own husband was too wrapped up to even notice her sitting beside him?

This isn't right.

After that, she knew what she had to do. Though revealing all her cards at once wasn't something Halsey Ambrosius generally advocated, it was the only option she had left.

She plunged her hand into her right jacket pocket, grabbed the copper orb, and pulled it out.

If they hate me after this, I can live with that. At least they won't end up killing each other over a lie my *family started by keeping the most important things secret for so long.*

The copper orb flashed with its internal golden light, growing slightly warmer in her palm as it responded to her emotions and her determination to stop this battle between the Clans. To repair some of the rifts that had cracked wide open between them all far before Halsey was even old enough to be aware of it.

The copper orb's magic blended with hers, bringing a

surprising amount of calm and clarity settling over her shoulders like a warm blanket. At the same time, all that combined magic further stoked the fires of her anger, annoyance, regret, and a touch of fear about what would happen after she stepped in.

But she *had* to step in this time. No one else was going to.

She opened her palm and let the copper orb do whatever it wanted.

The artifact zipped from her hand to hover directly over the center of the picnic table. Then it released a blinding flash of light.

The raging argument came to an abrupt stop, and everyone looked at the strange object floating above them before the words Halsey hadn't planned to say came flying from her mouth in an echoing boom.

"Everybody shut the hell up, pull your heads out of your asses, and listen to me because *I wasn't fucking finished!*"

If the strange flash of gold light and a sharp crack like the beginning of a thunderclap weren't enough to get everyone's attention, the furiously shouted words of one small young woman among them did the trick.

Breathing heavily, Halsey stared back at just under a dozen different gazes eyeing her in surprise and concern. She had no idea what to say that could possibly follow on the heels of her unplanned and highly uncouth exclamation. But it had worked.

She wondered if she'd have to be the one to break the silence again before Seamus snorted and announced with a crooked smile, "Well, that'll do the trick."

Halsey forced herself not to look at him, or she was

sure she'd end up grinning and looking way too proud of herself. Which wouldn't have helped her attempts to look like an experienced monster hunter who knew what she was doing instead of another elemental kid who wasn't ready for a seat at the big table.

Clearly, she wasn't the only one who found Seamus' comment amusing. Fiona covered her mouth with a hand to hide a smile. When Halsey looked at her, the woman removed her hand with a straight face once more and offered the young Ambrosius elemental a nod of approval.

Okay. Two out of...what? Eleven Havalons? It's a start.

Now that she had everyone's attention, she had to keep going.

"First, I want to say that I generally don't like screaming at people, especially when things are important. It felt like the only way to stop what no one else seemed to notice was happening here, and I really, *really* need everyone at this table to listen to what I have to say." She didn't mean to, but her gaze fell for a moment longer on Liam as she added, "*Without* interrupting me. Please."

The Havalons sitting beside Liam sniggered and shot him exaggerated grimaces to poke fun at him. But the man wasn't looking at Halsey. He hadn't moved an inch after craning his neck back to look up at the copper orb hovering over the center of the table, his jaw slack and hanging open.

"Aye, of course," Cillian replied, watching her with wide eyes and a hint of amusement. "Apologies, Halsey. Ye hadn't the chance ta finish yer thought, and, uh...well, clearly it's important to ye that ye get it fully out. I understand."

Okay, sure, I had to flex a little magical muscle to get everybody to chill the hell out. But why does it feel like he's placating me right now?

Still, she wouldn't toss the opportunity to say what she had to say out the window. Whether the Havalons were paying attention because they were scared of what "the Alpha Hunter" was capable of or because they truly valued her potential contribution to the conversation.

"Thank you," she murmured, then realized Liam still hadn't stopped staring at the sphere. She needed to change that.

The second the thought entered her mind, the ball of transmuted magical sand responded instantly, like she knew it would. In a flashing blur of copper and gold, far too bright to be a reflection of the setting sunlight, the object darted toward her open palm and settled there soundlessly.

"First, though," Cillian continued, pointing a thick finger at the orb. "May I ask what the hell that thing is?"

"With all due respect, Cillian, I'll get to that later." Halsey closed her fingers around the orb and pocketed it again, grateful for a bit of showmanship tucked into the vast and mostly undiscovered possibilities of what her strange item could do.

Seamus and Fiona both looked at their Clan leader and the head of their smaller family unit, their eyes wide in disbelief, amusement, and curiosity to see how the largest member of the Havalon Clan would handle his request being relegated to the back of the line.

Halsey couldn't see Seamus' face, but Fiona's expression told her everything she needed to know.

He's not the kind of man to lose his shit when somebody talks to him like that. Doesn't mean he's not totally surprised when it happens. Except for maybe when it's coming from his wife and son.

Again, she held back a knowing smile stoked by the realization that she wouldn't be punished for speaking out like this. The Ambrosius Clan would have handled this much differently, and they had. But Halsey was with what she might as well call her second family now. If she had the guts to sit at their ad-hoc Council table, offer suggestions, and stand her ground when she wasn't being heard, the Havalons were more than happy to have her there too.

Now she had the greatest opportunity of her life to share what she knew, offer information no one else had, and be taken at her word. If it went the way she hoped it would, sharing a few more secrets—both the Ambrosius Clan's and her own—could change the spiraling trajectory toward destruction all elementals faced right now.

Right. No pressure or anything.

CHAPTER EIGHTEEN

Halsey remained standing as she dove into what she'd previously meant to tell this gathering without shining the spotlight directly on herself. She didn't particularly relish the feeling of having taken a "superior position" the way her Uncle Arthur did during Ambrosius Council meetings with his enormous chair on the extending platform mounted in the center of their Council room. However, doing so ensured a much smaller chance of being interrupted, talked over, or shoved aside.

More than that, what she genuinely wanted was to look at everyone sitting on both sides of the table, not only those across from her.

To her surprise, the entire gathering remained perfectly silent. Everyone eyed her with open anticipation without a hint of disdain or skepticism. Even the Grendiers looked incredibly eager to hear what she had to say. Somehow, that felt like a major win.

"Liam," she began, nodding at him because he'd finally gotten over the shock her orb had elicited. "You said my theory about these monsters made sense. Because it does. I get that it would naturally make most of us think back to the stories and records we've all read or heard about the great war, the Mother of Monsters being locked away, and what our ancestors had to do in order to achieve that. Meaning most of us didn't survive. That's the logical assumption based on what we've been told or could piece together from everything left behind by those who came before us."

She turned her attention to the aunt of Seamus', whom she could have called out for starting the interrupting scream-fest at the table. *If* anyone here was keeping score or trying to place blame. "And Moya, you made a valid point about that being a problem. Which it would be if there was absolutely nothing that survived the great war beyond the elemental families. But everything changes when I tell you that's simply not true."

"Which part?" Moya murmured. Though her eyebrows flickered together in confusion, there was no hint of anger or resentment at having been called out.

Halsey had challenged the status quo of elemental history for the last twenty thousand years, and now everyone rightfully expected her to support that challenge. Which she could.

"The part about our ancestors being the only ones who survived the Ice Age *they* created."

She let that hang in the air for a moment, gauging how well her rapt listeners were handling the claim as it sank into their awareness. No one looked like they were about to explode or fall apart, so she kept going.

"The monsters didn't survive the war, that's true. But

haven't any of you wondered *how* the things managed to make a comeback in the eighth century after so long in between? Honestly, I used to think it was just something that happened, like being born an elemental with magic and growing up to be a monster hunter. None of us sprang up out of thin air, though. It's all cause and effect. The *cause* of monsters returning in 953 A.D. *after* they were all wiped out was that someone else survived, too. A blood human."

Several elementals took sharp breaths in surprise. Some looked around the table to gauge their neighbors' reactions. Others simply stared at Halsey, waiting for her to continue her revelatory explanations before they said anything else. Both Cillian and Fiona were among those diligently watching her, and though neither reacted as much as the other elementals, it was obvious she'd captured their full attention.

Maybe because her words made sense or because they trusted this particular elemental. It didn't matter *why* they listened as long as they did.

Fortunately, she didn't have to talk over anyone, and she didn't need curious questions to prompt her to continue. Whatever questions this gathering might have asked, she'd already been through countless times in her own mind. She hadn't realized how prepared she was for this until she dove in again.

"I know it sounds impossible. I know it goes against everything we thought we knew about our history and monsters. But I also know it's the truth." She inhaled and scanned their faces, gathering her courage. Now that she'd opened this door, she had to walk through it. The only small problem was that this particular door opened into the landmine of the Ambrosius Clan's family secrets and all the less-than-stellar choices they'd made over the last several decades in order to *keep* those secrets.

"My grandmother, Greta Ambrosius, found proof of this twenty years ago in our Clan Library. Our ancestor Cedric penned an eyewitness account of a discovery he made with five other elementals of the time. From the Havalon Clan, the Grendier Clan, and members of three other Clans who had also survived the great war and were still around. In the eighth century, at least."

That little factoid got her several confused frowns, which Halsey understood. The other Clans were thought to have died out long before monsters had returned to the world because the Ambrosius, Havalon, and Grendier Clans were the only three who'd been fighting those monsters since. Somewhere along the way, either they'd lost track of the other Clans, or those who'd survived the great war could not sustain that survival and had died out. Either way that still wasn't the most important message.

"Cedric and his…companions, I guess, for lack of a better word. They found a crashed Viking longship on the shores of Ireland in 953 A.D. The same year the Ambrosius Clan's historical accounts of finding, fighting, and subduing monsters began. Before that, there hadn't been a single mention of them after the great war. If you all went back through your own Clan histories, I'd be willing to bet 953 is the year your families' accounts of monster hunting started, too.

"I know a wrecked ship doesn't sound all that convincing when we're talking about monsters and blood humans and history being a hell of a lot different than any of us thought. However, Cedric also wrote about what they found on the ship. Claw marks. Teeth marks. Feathers that didn't belong to any known bird. Shed skin, fangs, and holes in the thick wood that could only have been left by the kind of creatures we all know and love to hate. The ones with acid, anyway." She lifted a hand to mime an explosive spray, then instantly felt like an idiot for thinking her audience didn't already know what she was talking about.

You're not narrating a presentation, Hal. Come on. Hands down.

Yet the levity the motion brought to her words made some of the Havalons chuckle. They all knew what she meant by particularly disliking the supernatural beasts who could melt the flesh off their bones simply by hissing at them with incredible aim.

When she darted a glance at Seamus, he was already grinning. He raised his eyebrows and nodded down the length of the table without breaking his gaze.

There's no way that doesn't mean "keep going." Well, thanks, Seamus. I think.

Halsey wasn't as successful this time at hiding her smile, but she shook it off and returned to her explanation. "I know that's a pretty big stretch. A shipwrecked Viking ship beaten up by signs all of *us* would recognize as monster markings but could also have been made by any number of wild animals who'd found the remains. Pair that with the same year my Clan's accounts of hunting and cataloging creatures? No. It doesn't seal the deal on the theory.

"Neither does the fact that Cedric and the other

elementals with him also found a dead monk on the ship. No name. No way to identify him. Only a hole in his belly where he'd probably been run through by a sword. It *is* strange that the monk's body was untouched while the rest of the ship had clearly been destroyed, but no. Still not enough to prove anything. I get that, too.

"It wasn't only a ship and a monk, though. They also found a scroll on that ship. Covered in blood runes. This part's conjecture on my end, but if anyone with any knowledge of blood runes had kept that scroll and deciphered it, they would have found an invocation there. A ritual spell. We all know only a blood human can read the magic of their own language, invoke it, and use it to do…well, all the terrible things they did before our ancestors banded together against the Blood Matriarch and wiped her children off the map. Except not *all* of them."

The varying expressions of interest, intrigue, rapidly working minds, and stubborn disbelief coming at her from all sides made her pause.

As she gathered her thoughts to keep going, Alvara raised a few fingers but didn't wait for permission to speak. "We would be most interested in studying this penned account for ourselves. Is this possible?"

Halsey grimaced, then briefly shook her head. "I'm sorry, no. My grandmother took it to the Order of Skrár, hoping they'd help her decipher a few other details, but… Actually, that's all part of a different story that may or may not actually have anything to do with what we're talking about right now. So I won't even get into that.

"I'll just say I know the record exists. Greta told me what was on it, and I trust her. It helps that the rest of the

Ambrosius Clan at the time had also seen Cedric's report, so there's no arguing that the crazy old lady made it all up. She didn't."

Another round of soft chuckling circled the table, though it skipped Alvara and Dietrich, who didn't get the amusement. The Havalon Clan knew what Greta Ambrosius was capable of and had said as much during Halsey's first visit to their home. Apparently, Greta hadn't fostered the same kind of cooperative friendship with the Grendier Clan.

"I also know the events Cedric wrote about in his account actually happened. I know they're tied to monsters returning to this world, to a blood human who'd escaped the war and managed to stay hidden, and to what's happening now to the monsters *we're* left to fight." A nervous laugh escaped her, and she figured it couldn't hurt to add more humor to the whole thing. "I know this is a lot to take in all at once, and I've *almost* gotten to the point. So just bear with me."

More smiles bloomed in response, and Cillian folded his hands on the picnic table before grinning and giving her a curt nod to continue.

This is where shit gets weird 'cause it's not simple history anymore. Not ancient history, anyway. Far more recent.

While holding the Clan leader's gaze, Halsey returned the nod and continued, speaking directly to him because it felt like the right thing to do. The thing she *should* have done before leaving Ireland and letting the entire Havalon Clan call her the Alpha Hunter.

"I don't think it would've been possible to make these connections if I hadn't...experienced something I honestly didn't want to believe or even talk about the last time I was here. I'm sure everybody remembers *that* werewolf hunt..."

"Aye."

"Bloody bastards."

"Nothin' against the Alpha Hunter."

She had no idea who'd made the last comment, and while it elicited several laughs and nods all around, it made Halsey uncomfortable. She could only manage a tight smile that felt like a pained grimace. But she had to acknowledge what had happened and that she was probably about to change their opinion of her after they heard the whole story.

Keeping lies and secrets for twenty years is what an Ambrosius used to do, Hal. A few months is still bad, but you can break that cycle right now. There's nobody here to stop you.

"I did kill the alpha," she started. "Not because I meant to, though. Not sure if you guys picked up on it, but *killing* monsters isn't really my thing, despite the fact that I've done quite a bit of it in the last few months. I didn't want to. I didn't even do it because the *alpha* wanted me to..."

Another pause came naturally there because, of course, no one could have heard her mention what a monster *wanted* from her and actually believe she'd meant to say that. Several confused frowns darkened several faces, but the silent promise the Havalon Council had made to hear her entire story wasn't broken.

"Um...yeah." Halsey glanced down at the end of the table and laughed. "I didn't misspeak right there. I tracked the alpha. We were alone, and it...he...spoke to me. I know it sounds crazy. But alphas have always been different than the rest of their species and the generations they spawned, right?

"I didn't tell any of you about it because it *does* sound insane. It makes *me* sound insane. But that alpha, with his dying breath, gave me the one thing I didn't know I needed to hear. The thing that would later prove *everything* I've been trying to warn my own Clan about for so long. Everything Brigham and I brought to your Council the last time we were here. And more than that now, obviously."

A lump formed in her throat. She might have given up on this entire endeavor if the looks from every elemental at the table hadn't so openly, authentically encouraged her to continue. No anger at discovering more secrets that had been kept from them. No resentment. No writing her off as another Ambrosius who warped the truth and pushed away everyone who cared about her.

This was it.

"The silverback alpha wanted me to kill him. I was stubborn enough to try not to, but he was strong enough to force me. It had to be one of us, and I only made the decision because...well, only one of us *didn't* want to die.

"But before he was gone, he told me plenty. The man he once was called himself Rolfr Magnusson. He told me he'd already tried to stop her once. That he thought he had. He'd resigned himself to living forever, apparently, because that was his price to pay for what he was. But this man inside the beast *knew* the Mother of Monsters had returned. And even the very first werewolf in this world couldn't stand to live through it. Which says a lot about what we're all facing right now. So that's fun."

The soft rise of polite laughter surprised her enough

that she searched for those who'd made the sound, though it could have been anyone.

Stay focused. You already know these guys have a weird sense of humor, so roll with it. They're listening.

"So. Alphas." Halsey cleared her throat and punched a fist into her palm in an attempt to refresh her memory. The final pieces were coming together, and if she didn't lay them out now, she might as well have wasted all their time. "Rolfr Magnusson. He told me all this as he was dying with my axe in his chest. He told me to remember his name. That he'd tried to atone for…whatever he might have done in his previous life, I guess. The one without fur and fangs. But the last thing he said to me… Well. I had to do some digging to figure it out, but now I know. And it changes everything."

She called up the redheaded Viking's last words exactly as he'd spoken them, knowing now what they were and what they meant after hours of puzzling together sounds, dead languages, and their meanings.

"'*Munkurinn hafdi rétt fyrir sér*,'" she repeated with a nod. Though she didn't glance at him again, she felt Seamus look sharply at her after hearing the quote. *He remembers me telling him about it, doesn't he? He just didn't know I'd heard it from a dying alpha werewolf. Because who the hell would believe something like that unless it's literally the only viable option left and ties the whole damn kaboodle together?*

She'd have to explain her little white lie to Seamus, too. Later. When she finished this nerve-racking presentation which had way more riding on it than she could possibly imagine right now.

"Those were the man's final words," Halsey added

quickly. "The beast's too, I guess. It took me way longer than I wanted to figure out what it meant. Which probably had something to do with the fact that it's Old Norse. Language of the Vikings. The mother tongue he reverted to when he...saw the light. Or whatever. One can only hope."

After taking a deep breath and steadying herself against the memory of those last few moments with the alpha, she puffed it all out in a reassuring sigh and plodded onward to wrap this whole thing up.

"It means, 'The monk was right.'"

She paused again to scan the Council's reactions and almost burst out laughing.

Oh, yeah. Fucking jackpot.

She spread her arms and shrugged. "I'm sure you guys don't need me to connect all the dots here for you, but I kinda have to..." Her gaze fell on the Grendier siblings, who'd listened with as much rapt attention and hungry anticipation as the Havalons. Minus Alvara's single inquiry about Cedric's personal account. "Feel free to take this right back to your own Council when you go because I *really* don't wanna have to tell this story all over again."

Some of the Havalons sniggered and failed to hide louder amusement. Dietrich pursed his lips, which could have meant anything, but he didn't argue. His sister, however, graced the young Ambrosius elemental with a closed-lipped smile that instantly softened her features.

All right. Scoring some serious points here. Finally.

"So." Tipping her arms up and down like balancing scales, Halsey glanced at the sunset sky bursting with orange, pink, and purple as a backdrop to the Havalon

Clan's merrymaking. Somehow, the view felt like a fresh start.

"The monk was right. The dying Viking said so. That wrecked longship was Rolfr Magnusson's ship. The dead monk found there with a blood-rune spell was 'the monk who was right' about *something*. And the silverback alpha recognized the silver coffin my cousin Brigham and I found on the beaches of Moher during this last summer solstice. The alpha was there that night, too, under a full moon. We saw him. He called his pack away from us and the coffin, which was weird enough on its own, but now I know why he did.

"Because I also know, like in my *bones*, it was the same coffin he tossed back into the sea in 953 while his crew went mad and turned into beasts, and the Mother of Monsters brought back some of her children. The same year my Clan started fighting monsters in this world again and writing about it.

"Now, obviously, I can't speak for the rest of you. But I would rather take the word of *the* first werewolf since the great war over…whew. Over *all* the denial that's been circulating around this theory lately. And Rolfr Magnusson's word isn't even part of ancient history or another bedtime story. He gave it to *me*. Personally. In the process of me taking his life and…I don't know. Givin' a wolfman what he wanted, I guess."

She tossed her arms in exasperation because she couldn't find the words to describe *everything* about that night the way they'd happened, the way it had felt, without breaking into tears. There weren't any tears, but the wry humor intended to ease her own discomfort served as another icebreaker for her enraptured audience.

Apparently, it was something both Grendier siblings could find humor in this time.

Yeah. Funny now. Wait 'til the whole thing sinks in, though.

"All that's only one part of the problem here, isn't it?" she added before the soft laughter died down. "The only thing my long and complicated story achieves is to prove two things. The Blood Matriarch is back. She's the one *causing* all the weird changes in monsters, and knowing that doesn't help us beyond the fact that sometimes, thinking about *that* part scares me shitless.

"The second thing is that a *few* blood humans made it through the great war without any of our ancestors knowing about it. They stayed hidden. They waited for… whatever variables were *just right* the night that blood spell was cast aboard Rolfr Magnusson's longship. A blood human was on that ship. Maybe it was the monk. Maybe not. I can admit I don't know everything.

"But if blood humans made it through the great war, the Ice Age, and centuries of hiding from elementals who would've wiped them out in a second, it makes all the sense in the world that one or two of the strongest, smartest, fastest, most *evolved* creatures from before the war might have made it through. Might've waited even longer than the blood human who freed his matriarch from the sea. Hell, those monsters could've been watching *us*. Learning about elementals, biding their time until we all got so fucking wrapped up in who's right and who's wrong that we—"

Seamus blatantly forced a cough, instantly clearing

Halsey's mind. She cast him a reproving frown before realizing why he'd tried to steer her back on track.

"Sorry." She looked at the other faces around the table and laughed. "Sometimes I get carried away. Nobody wants to sit around and be lectured about all the doom-and-gloom shit, so. Uh…I guess that's everything. Thanks."

Halsey stepped stiffly back toward the end of the picnic bench and plopped into her empty seat. Her entire body burned from head to toe, and she hoped to whatever gods of magic existed that she wasn't blushing as furiously as she felt like she was.

She continued to sit there, not quite daring to look at anyone else. All she could do was wait, feeling like an idiot because she clearly hadn't rehearsed a closing statement as much as she'd run through all the important facts of her little speech.

Whatever happened after this, it was out of her hands.

For once, that was actually a relief.

CHAPTER NINETEEN

The silence around the backyard picnic table was almost deafening, even with the background drone of the other Havalons laughing, drinking, eating, talking, and playing all around them as if everything was right in the world.

They'd probably be right about that. The way they stay so close to each other and so happy all the time? It's all just as important as the seriously shitty stuff every Clan's facing right now, whether we like it or not. Hopefully, we keep facing it together. That's the only way any of us are gonna get through this to the other side. Whatever the hell that turns out to be...

At first, she thought the silence was from the spell of utter shock she'd cast over the gathering. Maybe they all needed more time to let the words soak in and gather their thoughts before the next wave of emotion. Or, at the least, someone would tell her it was an interesting story and thank her for sharing, they would take it under consideration, now let the grownups get back to work.

Yet no one said a thing.

So it didn't go as poorly as I thought. It's so much worse.

Seamus nudged her boot under the table again, and she subtly kicked his foot aside with enough pressure to get her point across but not hog the limelight all over again. She didn't want to look at anyone.

The nudge caught her a second time, and because Halsey was already at the end of her rope with just about everything, she whipped her head up and hissed, *"What?"*

Fighting back a smile without moving his head, Seamus flicked his gaze to his left, down the line of the six other elementals on his side of the table.

When she glanced in the same direction, she found literally everyone staring at her, including Cillian and Fiona. The Havalon Council head was grinning at her.

Great. I'm the crazy Ambrosius who shows up out of the blue to scream at people with my weird magical ball, babble about talking werewolves, and act like a little shit when somebody's trying to get my attention. You're taking on way too much at once, Halsey. Gotta let some of it go.

She forced herself to hold the Clan leader's gaze and swallowed.

"Once again, lass," he began, his voice booming inside of the magical soundproof barrier. "Ye've made yerself even *more* invaluable. And ye have our thanks."

"I..." Her mouth popped open and stayed like that because she couldn't think of anything else to say.

"Alvara? Dietrich?" Cillian turned toward the Grendier siblings and raised an eyebrow. "Will Halsey's explanation for the creatures you're huntin' be sufficient enough ta take back ta yer Clan and help with yer search?"

The blond elementals exchanged a knowing look and came to a mutual decision without saying a word.

Alvara nodded. "This is most illuminating information, yes. Our Council will be pleased with this, whether or not such a theory leads to more success with these monsters than we've previously had. There is more than enough here to properly prepare and arm ourselves. Miss Ambrosius?"

Halsey blinked and had to lean forward to see past everyone sitting between her and the Grendier woman. When their gazes met, she found herself staring into another pair of intense blue eyes. Not deep, sparkling blue like Seamus' but a lighter, icy blue, as if the Grendier Clan's much colder climates had bred the color out of each generation's eyes and hair.

Alvara offered her a warm smile tinged with something that looked like sadness, and Halsey would never have understood the expression if the woman's words hadn't put meaning to them. "Young woman, I must say I did not expect any Ambrosius elemental to be here at such a meeting. Now or in the foreseeable future, to be honest."

Despite her previous fear that she'd done nothing but make a complete fool of herself, Halsey replied on autopilot. "Totally understandable, Alvara. I'm not just any Ambrosius, though."

Dietrich roared with laughter and pounded the picnic table with an open hand.

"Indeed you are not," his sister agreed over his snorting cackles. "You are very young to carry the weight of so much knowledge and experience on your shoulders. But not too young to use that knowledge for the best possible good. I understand personally how difficult of a situation our current circumstances have forced you into. And on behalf of the Grendier Clan, I wish to thank you for what you have shared with all of us today."

Someone else at the table snorted and muttered, "Bet she never thought she'd be sayin' *that* to an Ambrosius, eh?"

Alvara ignored him like everyone else and nodded at Halsey. "Rest assured, you will not be required to repeat your stories or the conclusions to which they have led you. Though I do hope it is not too forward of me to ask for a preferred method of contact, should the Grendier Council wish to consult with you regarding any of our next steps in this…new war we all face."

"Method of contact?" Halsey echoed, her mouth falling open.

"Yours, yes. *If* you approve, of course. I believe you may be a valuable resource for all of us in the coming months, and while we have other ways to contact other members of your Clan, we… Well. How do I put this lightly?"

"You'd rather talk to an Ambrosius you've met in person and can trust?" Halsey finished with a smirk. "I think there's a line for that somewhere, right?"

More laughter circled the table, and it finally sounded like real laughter now. Airy, light, jovial, and above all, filled with relief. Neither the Grendiers' trip to Ireland nor the Havalons' *cruinniú* had been in vain. No one would have to return to their regular lives after this with nothing to show for it. No one would leave this table feeling impotent with a lack of knowledge or direction.

They weren't completely powerless after all.

Amid the laughter, Halsey nodded at the blonde woman, intending to hand over a working email address at some point tonight before they all parted ways. Alvara looked incredibly pleased by this. Her brother didn't seem to care one way or the other, though his gaze did frequently return to Halsey's jacket pocket.

If he wanted another peek at the copper orb, it wasn't happening right now.

Shit. I told Cillian I'd explain that one, and I totally forgot.

Halsey opened her mouth to bring it up to him, which was the least she could do after effectively dismissing him the first time, then receiving all the unwavering attention from his entire Council during the entire length of her storytelling.

She didn't have a chance.

"All interestin' surprises aside," Cillian boomed through another laugh. "I'd say that went fairly well. Now we've all got just the right amount 'o knowledge necessary ta help each other move forward. I, for one, meant ta move forward with the rest o' the night. And, of course, our guests're always welcome ta join us."

As the first one to finally take his plastic cup of whiskey in hand, which Halsey assumed was what everyone else had been waiting for, the Havalon Clan leader raised it for a toast while trying to keep from laughing too hard. "Ta protectin' a world that'll never know a thing!"

Everyone else grabbed their cups and raised them as well, all eyes on Cillian. He spared a glance for every one of them, finishing with Halsey, and shot her another wink. "*Slainte.*"

Then he downed the small cup's entire contents.

"*Slainte.*"

The Irish toast echoed in over a dozen voices and sealed the deal on the end of the Council meeting that felt more casual than anything Halsey's family did and, at the same time, seemed to carry so much more ritual and ceremony. There was no telling what a Grendier Clan Council meeting looked like. Yet somehow, Halsey suspected the European Clan was slightly more formal and fell somewhere in the middle when it came to democracy.

Gathering together. Sharing information. Working as a community for a common cause without pitting Clan against Clan and family member against family member.

For the first time in a long time, members of all three elemental families sat together at the same table, toasting over tiny plastic cups of neat Irish whiskey. Halsey echoed the toast as loudly and enthusiastically as anyone, the cup already at her lips before the word had fully emerged from her mouth.

She knocked back the whole thing at once like everyone else around the table.

Then she forced back a cough, slammed her cup down, wheezed, and stared at Seamus with wide eyes.

He smacked his lips and grinned. "That's good stuff, right there."

"Yep…" Instead of trying to talk through the burn, she let it fizzle out on its way into her stomach, immediately followed by a similar sensation at the top of her head. She couldn't help but grin as the other Havalons burst out laughing and began to rise from their seats.

"That's the end o' that fer the night," Cillian called. "Grendiers! Stay as long as ye like. Our home is yers. Nothin' barred, nothin' forbidden. Now, there better be enough supper left on that table, or so help me…"

Standing with everyone else, Halsey fully appreciated

the subtlety of the table becoming simply another picnic table again. She picked up her empty whiskey glass, studied it more closely, and laughed when she realized it had probably held two shots' worth, if not more. "You know, it would've been *super* nice to have this before I stood up and gave that whole stupid…"

Not knowing exactly what to call it, she puffed out a sigh and set the cup down.

Seamus walked around the end of the table toward her with a grin. "Ye mean yer formal address?" He laughed when she shot him an exasperated glare, but even she couldn't keep from smiling at the good-natured joke. "Aye, t'would've made it far easier. Fer the one speakin', anyhow. But ye didn't *need* it, and that's the point. Bit of an old trick for figurin' out who can handle themselves in a tight spot 'n who can't. I've only ever seen two people grab one o' those cups before it was time." He leaned toward her until his mouth was beside her ear and whispered, "And they never came back ta the table."

Halsey laughed, and it felt more genuine, real, and cleansing than any positive emotion she'd experienced in what seemed like an incredibly long time.

She hadn't known sharing her secrets and her fears not only with Seamus but with the whole Havalon Clan, plus two auspiciously timed Grendier Clan visitors, would be something of a final test for her. Breaking her family's cycles. Stopping the lies and the secrets. Offering up information technically unasked for but vital for the survival of every elemental. Probably humanity as a whole too.

Though the Mother of Monsters hadn't technically been spotted, and none of the elemental Clans knew where to look for her or how they would come together to defeat her, it gave Halsey some comfort to know they were following in their ancestors' footsteps.

The number of elementals alive in this world and willing to fight for it was far fewer than twenty thousand years ago when they waged war against the Blood Matriarch, her blood priests and blood humans, and all the other monsters they'd created with their taboo magic. No one could argue that fact. But the three remaining elemental Clans still had an advantage over the enemy they'd never expected to face in their lifetimes.

They had the knowledge and resources of their past. They had the ability to learn from their ancestors' victories —and their mistakes—to steer them down the right path. They had centuries of experience living, working, and thriving in the modern world. Existing *among* the humans they'd been tasked to protect while also battling the Blood Matriarch's beastly offspring.

And they had each other.

More than anything, that would carry the elementals through the coming darkness. No matter what it looked like or what they would have to sacrifice in order to come out of it.

Until today, Halsey had always considered the collaborative mindset of "teamwork" and strength in unity more an ethereal idea than a possibility. The Ambrosius Clan had forgotten the strength in that unity and why it was so vital in preserving their way of life and the safety of the human population.

Halsey's family had never taught her these things. Tonight, she knew she'd found the meaning of it anyway.

She'd shared a *cruinniú* table with the Havalon Clan as one of their own, accepted fully and completely. She'd deliberated with their Council and two Grendier elementals brave enough to step forward and risk the consequences of going against their Council's orders.

And she'd been taken seriously, at her word. Without hesitation, suspicion, or any of her words being colored by the mistakes of others' past.

The *cruinniú* couldn't have gone any better. Whatever sort of true test it had been, Halsey knew she had passed.

Which meant that from here on out, even though she had no idea what it would look like, she'd regained her confidence in the Clans' ability to trust each other. To work together and do what had to be done.

She gazed into Seamus Havalon's eyes and spread her arms. "So we can get to the party now, right?"

He laughed and gestured toward literally anywhere else on the open lawn. "It's yer party as much as it is any of ours, Hal."

"Excellent." She reached for her plastic cup. "Let's start with some drinks—"

"Leave the cup where ye set it." With a gentle hand, he grabbed her wrist to stop her and nodded. "It's had its use fer tonight. I'm happy to fetch ye somethin' from the taproom if ye're truly in that much need."

"I think I might be." Seamus' gleaming grin winked at her in the steadily growing darkness, and he released her wrist to take her hand instead. "You know, a few pints after the airport were great, but I hope you can tell me there's more whiskey."

His mouth popped open in mock insult as he leaned

away from her. "More whiskey? O' *course* there's more. What d'ye think we are, Hal? Savages?"

"Well, you certainly have your moments."

Laughing, he tugged her along as they headed across the lawn to join the Havalon Clan's nightly festivities.

Halsey was able to truly let herself enjoy the moment without constantly trying to shove aside whatever happened to be hanging over her head. Tonight, everything was right with the world, and that was all she needed to know.

CHAPTER TWENTY

Despite the evening's harrowing discoveries and the ensuing implications, the festive air billowing throughout the Havalon Clan estate exploded tenfold when the Council members, their two foreign guests, and Halsey and Seamus ended their meeting. In true Havalon fashion, the night continued as one giant party to celebrate the mere fact that they were all alive and well and physically capable of gathering.

Once again, Halsey was surprised by the extreme value this family placed on transparency, honesty, and making sure everyone was brought into the loop about the most important things. Multiple times throughout the night, she overheard various Council members summarizing what was discussed at the meeting before giving instructions to make sure the entire Clan had heard the news.

Some of the other elementals approached her personally to satiate their curiosity with questions of their own.

Had she spoken to the Order of Skrár about the record of the Viking longship Greta had found?

Who else in her Clan knew this information?

Did Halsey want help bringing her family together so they could all have the necessary information, even if that meant they'd have to deal with seeing the Havalons again?

Could they start an email chain for small communications so she wouldn't have to deal with this all over again?

Did the silverback alpha actually move his lips when he spoke to her as a werewolf?

Was she going to move to Ireland and settle down with Seamus, or what?

Under normal circumstances, Halsey would have felt bombarded and overwhelmed by so many questions across such a broad range of topics. She would have tried to get out somehow to feel like she could breathe again. Yet after how well the meeting had gone and how completely the Havalons had accepted her into the fold, she didn't mind any of it. She laughed at the jokes, parried with a few of her own, gave straightforward answers wherever possible, and tried not to read into what any of it meant.

The food laid out on the banquet tables seemed neverending. Drinks were refilled and passed around more often than she could keep track of. A five-Havalon band broke out their instruments to entertain with their own renditions of modern songs interspersed with old Irish shanties, drinking songs, and love ballads. Then people started to loosen up, and the back lawn became a massive dance floor covered in soft, lush grass beneath a black swath of nighttime sky studded with a splash of brilliant stars.

Seamus finally cajoled her into a dance to the jaunty tune of an Irish song. While she had no idea how to dance *anything*, let alone an Irish jig, the sight of the incredibly tall, broad-shouldered, grinning elemental bouncing to the music amused her.

At one point, Dietrich approached Halsey to get her email address and to thank her again for what she'd done for all the Clans. "I meant every word of what I said, Halsey. If you find yourself in need of anything at all, call me at this number. You will not find it in our more…public list of Clan contact information. I always answer."

"Thank you." Halsey humbly accepted the small, sparsely decorated business card with nothing but the woman's name and phone number embossed on the front.

"It did not feel like the appropriate time to ask during the meeting," the woman continued with a soft smile, studying Halsey's face. "I am curious to know how an Ambrosius came to be here in Ireland. I would never have known you belonged to any other Clan if you had not freely expressed it yourself."

"How did I get here?" Halsey puffed a sigh that turned into a carefree chuckle. "That's a long story. I guess the short version is I was looking for answers on my own because it seemed like the only way I would find anything. My cousin Brigham was with me the first time. He's back in Texas now. It wasn't because of official orders or a mission if that's what you're wondering." She slowly looked around the back lawn, the whole area studded with tiny lights, both artificial and magical, to ward off the darkness, then shrugged. "I guess this is the place to go for *anyone* who's looking for answers."

Alvara broke into another warm, gracious smile that softened her harsh features. "It would seem so. I am grateful we could both find them here. Perhaps this may help you find them elsewhere, too, should the need arise."

She held out her palm to offer Halsey one of the smaller pieces of the shattered glass-like substance that had come from the mystery monsters. Halsey took it with a soft smile and managed to hide her surprise and growing curiosity when the smooth material sent a soft, buzzing jolt of energy through her palm and up into her arm. It faded before she pocketed the thing, making sure not to stick it in the same pocket as the copper orb.

If that was something everybody felt, the Grendiers would've mentioned it by now. Looks like it's only me, then. Again.

"Thank you," she murmured and left it at that.

With another gracious nod, the woman left Halsey in search of more food or drinks, or possibly her brother. Which also meant Halsey was momentarily left alone with her thoughts as well.

Yeah, Brigham was here with me the first time. Now he's not. I have a lot of explaining to do when I get home, but I do know he's safe. And he definitely knows I'm here.

Giving herself only a brief moment to satiate her curiosity, she pulled out her phone to check for messages. There were none. Her cousin hadn't called or texted, and the Ambrosius Council hadn't tried to make contact. Beyond that, there was no one else she would have wanted to hear from anyway.

You talked to him last yesterday, Halsey. He's probably still settling in, jetlagged as hell, and leaving you alone because you said you were going to Ireland to be with Seamus. That's it.

It made sense, and nothing nagged at her in the back of her mind about it. So she slipped the phone back into her pocket and answered a summons from the closest group of Havalons, who wanted a moment to talk and laugh and visit with her. Not as the Alpha Hunter but as Halsey Ambrosius. She couldn't say no to that.

She didn't talk to either of the Grendier siblings after that. As the night wore on and she realized she hadn't seen them since her short conversation with the blonde woman, she assumed they'd left the party, if not the Havalon estate itself. But the late hour, the amount of drinks being passed around, and the shared ordeal of the meeting made it more likely the Grendiers had accepted their hosts' offer to put them up in one of the various rooms the Havalons kept open and ready for guests.

Halsey wasn't tired, though. Not even close.

Eventually, when the older kids and some of the teenagers had settled down for the night, the party moved into the common room of the big house. Someone had already set a fire in the enormous hearth. More drinks were passed around, and Halsey and Seamus found themselves sitting on a couch in front of the fire, drinks in their hands and his arm slung around her shoulders.

"Might not've been the type o' visit ye expected," he told her with a crooked smile. "But I'm glad ye're here."

"Yeah, me too. I needed this." She sucked in a breath and widened her eyes. "Like…badly." They both laughed, neither one of them needing to mention her little episode on the side of the highway or the many details she'd revealed at the *cruinniú* that she'd chosen not to share with him before. He didn't have to say it, but she knew Seamus didn't need or even want an explanation from her. Right now, it didn't feel important.

What did feel important was making sure he knew how much all of this meant to her, especially now. "So thank you, Seamus," she added softly. "For everything."

"Ah, don't mention it." He hugged her closer and added through a smirk, "Only know the next time I find myself in a sudden emergency, ye're the one I'm callin' ta help me out of it."

"Ha! Fair enough."

It was a surprising relief to realize they could sit here and enjoy the night for what it was without having to talk about anything or dive into answering questions and putting pieces together. Seamus was content with the present, which Halsey appreciated more than she thought she might.

His dad, on the other hand, wasn't nearly as casual about leaving what he did and didn't know for a later time.

A round of boisterous laughter erupted from the opposite side of the room, then Cillian emerged from the center of a larger group of Havalons. A few of them clapped him good-naturedly on the back as they laughed and let him pass.

"Been a good night for him, too," Seamus muttered as they watched his dad pause to slug back whatever he'd poured into his mug.

"Specifically, or in general?" Halsey asked. She'd meant it as a joke, but when she looked at Seamus, his brief flicker of concern didn't escape her notice.

"Nae, he generally has good nights. One right after the other." He tried to lighten the mood with a smile, but he couldn't take his eyes off his dad. "Today, though? Honestly, it's been a long time since I've seen him look as worried as he did sittin' at that table. Knew somethin' was wrong the second I caught sight of his face. But I think ye managed brilliantly ta help him pull himself back together in the end. He's like ta thank ye fer it himself, but in case he doesn't... Thank ye, Hal. Ye did a good thing tonight. Fer all of us. Don't forget that, aye?"

"Trust me. This is the kinda night that's especially hard to forget."

It was true in more ways than one. She didn't have the time to process what that meant or share it with the handsome, dark-haired Irishman beside her because Cillian Havalon had crossed the common room, laughing and stumbling only once despite the enormous volume of drinks he'd consumed. Red-faced and grinning, the Clan leader made it safely onto the area rug beneath the coffee table in front of the two young elementals. They both watched him in amusement, and Halsey wondered if this was the part of the celebration where Cillian called it a night, and everything else sort of fizzled out.

She hadn't stuck around long enough last time to figure it out.

But Cillian then raised his empty cup toward his son and Halsey, his green eyes winking in the overhead light and the fire's glow. Most of the gaiety smoothed from his face into a small, warm smile as he gazed at them. When he dipped his head and bowed at the waist, he moved like a man entirely sober. And incredibly formal for the setting.

Halsey stifled a laugh, and Seamus chuckled at his dad's display. "Havin' yerself a time, there, Da?"

Still bent over in his bow, Cillian whipped his head up toward them and grinned. "Oh, aye." He lurched violently upright without stumbling or swaying, lifted his empty cup, and bellowed, "Ta the young and fearless! May they continue ta laugh at their elders but ne'er be the ones ta knock 'em over!"

A round of laughter and shouted agreement rang from every part of the common room as other Havalons joined the toast and thrust various drinks into the air.

Halsey looked at Seamus and murmured, "What does that mean, exactly?"

He chuckled and shook his head. "He's the only one who knows right now. Come the mornin', though... Well, I've stopped askin'."

She laughed and tried to stifle it when she realized Cillian was watching them again.

Looking proud of himself, the head of the Havalon Council fixed her with a compassionate smile. Sparkling drops of whatever had been in his mug flecked his black beard and mustache. "Look at the two o' ye. Warms my heart."

"It's sure ta do that, Da." Seamus nodded toward the enormous hearth in the wall. "Ye're nearly standin' *in* the fire."

Cillian turned to double-check that he was not as close to the hearth as his son would have him think, then chuckled. "Oh, aye! Is that all it is, then? Yet think ye have me beat, lad? Just ye wait." The man shuffled around the coffee table, then slowly settled into the armchair beside Halsey and Seamus' couch. He bent his legs as far as he could and grunted before falling onto the chair's cushion. "Just ye wait..."

Halsey and Seamus watched his dad with cautious amusement.

Might get weird if the big guy decides he wants to pass out in his chair.

The young Havalon was apparently thinking along the same lines when he asked, "Ye want me ta fetch ya somethin' else, Da? Glass o' water, maybe?"

"No, no." Cillian waved off the suggestion and puffed a sigh between loose lips. "Yer Ma's bringin' a little somethin' out fer me. She'll be joinin' us soon." He chuckled. While his motions were wide, sweeping, and languid, as expected from someone who'd had plenty to drink, he didn't slur his words. And when he sat back and locked his gaze with Halsey's, his eyes were as clear and lucid as any other time she'd seen them.

"Thrilled ta see ye havin' yerself such a time, Halsey," he continued, his gaze unwavering. "Truly. But before the night comes to a close fer all of us, I believe there's one other thing needs a wee more explainin'."

CHAPTER TWENTY-ONE

She silently held his gaze, waiting for the man to continue with whatever this one other thing might be. When the silence hung on a little too long, she felt like she'd missed something.

"Da?" Seamus prompted.

Cillian's gaze flickered toward Halsey's jacket pocket, and he nodded slowly. "Aye, one last thing. Figured it's late enough ta count as later, don't ye think?"

"Oh." Her hand immediately went to her pocket and the small lump of copper orb. "I did say I'd get to it later, didn't I?"

"Ye did at that. And now ye won't have an audience of buggy eyes oglin' ye from across the way. Most of the bairns're long in their beds. Though ye may get a wee bit more attention from Liam than ye bargained for." The man threw his head back and shouted across the room, "Isn't that right, Liam?"

"Piss off!"

The reply garnered another vibrant round of laughter.

Cillian's booming voice joined the amusement, then he grinned at Halsey and spread his arms. "If ye don't mind, lass. I'd have ye tell a bit more of yer tale. We both know ye've somethin' ta show along with it this time."

"Yes, we do." Smiling back at him, Halsey wrapped her fingers around the cool surface of the orb. "What good am I if I don't stick to my word, right?"

"Aw, I'm sure ye're good fer plenty, Alpha Hunter." The large man shot her another wink, but it hit her differently when accompanied by the new nickname she still couldn't bring herself to accept.

Her smile faded as she withdrew the sphere from her pocket, then set it in her lap and covered it with both hands.

Cillian looked back and forth between her hands and her face with an amused frown and tilted his head. "Don't tell me it's gone all shy now."

She knew it was meant as another joke, but she couldn't bring herself to laugh at this one. "Not one of the words I'd use to describe it, no. But before I dive into *that* whole thing, I want to apologize to you. To both of you." She looked at Seamus again and received nothing but confusion.

"Whatever fer, lass?" Cillian's smile remained as steadfast and unwavering as the clear, lucid gaze on her face. "Ye've got nothin' ta be apologizin' 'bout. Hell, it's been us givin' ye *our* thanks all night."

"I know that, and I appreciate it. But still." Another deep breath gave her fortitude and a few more seconds to figure out how she wanted to say this. "I *do* have something to apologize for. I lied to you. Your whole family. Everyone.

The last time I was here when we went after the werewolves... I didn't tell any of you what actually happened. Not all of it. Obviously, you know the truth now because I'd talked myself into a corner until I couldn't keep all the proof to myself anymore. I should've told you about the alpha that night, though. Your entire family has been so good to me. Better than..."

The sting of oncoming tears made her stop, and she choked it all back before something less appealing burst out of her.

Keep it together, Halsey. Own your mistakes. Clear the air. Move on. If they didn't throw you out after the meeting, they're not gonna suddenly change their minds now.

With his arm still around her shoulders, Seamus gave her a reassuring squeeze, and she huffed before continuing. "The Havalon Clan has done more for me in a few months than my own family has in the last twenty years. Maybe even more. None of you deserved to be lied to, but I was too worried about whether an entire second Clan would follow the first, call me crazy, and sweep me under the rug with everything else they didn't wanna look at. I know that's not who any of you are. And, you know..."

She looked slowly at Cillian, expecting to find disappointment on his face but not surprised to see none. "After hearing what actually happened that night with the alpha, I wouldn't blame you if you wanted to kill the whole Alpha Hunter thing and pretend that part never happened."

For a moment, the large man stared blankly at her. Then he smacked his lips and leaned forward, settling his forearms on his thighs. He clasped both hands around his empty mug. "Did ye follow that alpha through the hills, lass?"

"Yeah. We all did."

"Did ye corner him all by yer lonesome?"

Halsey's gaze darted toward the fireplace in confusion, then settled on his face again. "Well, not intentionally. I just—"

"Did ye wield the blade that stopped the heart o' both man and beast?"

She took a deep breath, stopped fidgeting, and nodded. "I did."

"Then there ye have it." Cillian spread his arms and straighten. "If ye think this Clan hands out titles as often as we hand out drinks, lass, that's on us fer not fully explainin' it to ye. Everythin' we've given ye, we gave because it was *earned*. No exceptions. And don't ye go forgettin' it."

A whispering laugh escaped her as she shook her head. "I'll work on it. Alpha Hunter kinda makes me seem full of myself, though, doesn't it? Knowing the whole thing was one giant accident?"

The man held her gaze for so long, with his brows furrowed in concentration, that she wondered if he'd gone off on some tangent in his mind. As she was about to ask if he was all right, Cillian leaned and nodded. "Fiona told me 'twas yer first."

Her first kill. Her first technically completed hunt from start to finish. Her first initiating step into a true elemental monster hunter, which her family had been urging her to take since she'd graduated from her training and picked up her weapons.

Her first true experience, hunter against monster, knowing that only one of them could live.

Halsey swallowed thickly and nodded.

"Aye." Cillian glanced at his son, and though she couldn't see the look that passed between them, Seamus gave her shoulder another squeeze before hugging her closer. "First kill's a hell of a thing. It's hard all around, lass. On the body, sure, but the mind 'n the heart aren't left out o' the equation, either. Does it get easier with time? Maybe. Depends on how ye wanna look at it, and ye're the only one who can decide that fer yerself. But the *name*?"

Inhaling deeply through his nose, the man scanned the common room and the other Havalons still enjoying their celebration. Then he laughed and set his empty mug on the armrest, holding it like a scepter in a king's hand. "Aye, the *name* ye earned. It's yers. And no, it doesn't make ye some self-centered windbag blusterin' 'round 'n screamin' o' yer victories. It's not all of what ye are, but it covers a good deal all the same.

"It's a hard thing ta end any life at all, Halsey. Stay away from anyone who says different. The way I see it, though, it's even harder ta end someone who's begging you fer it with all their bein'. Whether or not they look like a monster on the outside doesn't make a lick o' difference."

"Accident or no," Seamus added, a joking smile flickering across his lips as he fought to contain it. "Ye're still a badass, Hal. I think that's what he's sayin'."

Cillian clicked his tongue and gestured flippantly. "Or that."

They all shared a good laugh, and Halsey didn't have to pretend to find the amusement even in how much she'd worried what the Havalons would think of her. No one was being judged here, and that might have been the greatest relief of all.

It made following through on her promise to tell Cillian about the copper orb the way she'd told his son much easier.

Before she even had a chance to pull the orb from her lap, though, Fiona appeared seemingly out of nowhere. She carried a small tray, its surface covered with glasses and another bottle of alcohol. She grinned from ear to ear as she approached the little chatting circle of three to make it four. Then she paused, looked from one of them to the next, and chuckled. "Well, isn't *this* a sight?"

"Aye, but it's far better from over here." Laughing, Cillian swiped at his wife in an attempt to pull her closer.

The petite woman dodged his giant hand, expertly balancing her tray without disturbing its contents more than a slight rattle. "And ye'd be sulking all night if ye made me spill any o' these. Sit down 'n stay down."

Whether or not she'd had as much to drink as her husband, Fiona didn't seem any different than when she was sober. She didn't sway or stumble but set the tray on the coffee table, opened the unmarked bottle with the hollow *pop* of a cork, then poured four equal glasses. "I trust ye haven't been discussin' anythin' *too* important without me."

"O' course not, dear. We would never." Cillian's mischievous smile betrayed his words.

Undaunted and slightly amused, his wife brushed it off with a smirk before handing him the first small drink. "There ye are."

She passed one each to Halsey and Seamus over the table and finally took the last for herself.

Halsey sniffed at the amber liquor and tilted her head. "What's this?"

"Special brandy," Fiona replied, raising her eyebrows.

"Homemade," Seamus muttered.

"Did ye take anythin' off the sweets table, lass?" Cillian asked.

With all three of them staring expectantly at her, Halsey couldn't help but laugh. "No…"

"Excellent. Then this is dessert." The Clan leader raised his drink, followed by everyone else raising theirs, and a brief silence while they enjoyed the flavor.

Halsey smacked her lips and had to try twice before she could say, "That's fantastic."

"Ye're damn right it is. Now, drink up 'n tell me all 'bout that wee bauble o' yers."

CHAPTER TWENTY-TWO

With Seamus throwing in a few good-natured jokes or occasionally prompting her to explain minor details she might have forgotten for his parents' benefit, Halsey told Cillian and Fiona Havalon absolutely everything. Plus a few things she hadn't even shared with Seamus yet. It all tied into her confusion, fears, concerns, and curiosity about the copper orb she carried with her everywhere she went now.

She described how much stranger her monster-hunting missions had become, each one becoming more obscure and challenging than the next. She recounted her brief communication and attempts to meet with Halil Aydem of the Order of Skrár and how he'd blown her off repeatedly until their final meeting in London. She even touched on the startling truths Greta Ambrosius had revealed to both her and Brigham.

That everything she'd grown up knowing about her mother Gillian Ambrosius' death had been a cover-up.

That Gillian had been fighting for the truth Greta attempted to bring to the Council for years, and the Ambrosius Council had chosen not to deal with the facts and move forward. Instead, they'd tried to hide it all behind lies and half-truths, plus a few gross exaggerations and exiling Greta from the Council before banishing her from the estate house itself.

And, of course, she told them everything about the copper orb and what it could do. Divert attention or attract it, rip monsters apart, heal humans when nothing else would work, and now command swarms of grindylows, apparently. All these things were so intrinsically tied together that it was hard to pick out the "relevant" parts and leave the rest behind.

Her unplanned presentation at the *cruinniú* had proven that cherry-picking the facts and handing people only what she thought they wanted to hear wasn't doing anyone any favors. It was about time *one* Ambrosius started telling the whole truth, and that was what she intended to do.

It wasn't only the facts she laid out for them in her stories, though. For the first time since finding that silver coffin, Halsey finally had the opportunity to talk about how she was *handling* it all.

How she felt safer here with the Havalons than anywhere else in her life, with the exception of her Meemaw's house.

How it had become hard to trust anyone these days because everyone she wanted to trust seemed to carry some major secret that kept revealing itself in devastating ways.

How she'd been terrified to talk to anyone about what

the magic of the copper orb was doing to her. Not to mention the *new*, completely non-elemental magic it had awakened inside her. That she'd been able to physically and emotionally *feel* every bit of magic the orb worked, whether it was to destroy, to heal, or to create.

That she loved the shiny little sphere of copper-colored metal as much as it terrified her.

Most of all, she finally talked about what this new magic of hers might entail for the foreseeable future, including the eventual battle with the Mother of Monsters they all knew they would have to face. Would it be a blessing or a curse? Did the Blood Matriarch know this magic existed in elementals?

Should she allow herself to give into such powerful magic without knowing what it was, even if for the sole purpose of helping the elementals, saving those in need, and protecting those she cared about?

The Havalons didn't have answers for her most pressing questions, but they listened intently. And they didn't turn her away for the same confessions she expected her family's Council to lock her up over. *If* she chose to tell them.

When I choose to tell them. When. I have to. They deserve to know as much as anyone else, even if they want to keep pretending we're not all in this together.

After she'd let it all out for her attentive audience of three, Halsey shook her head and stared at the coffee table. "I know it's a lot. Most of it, I feel like I can accept and get over, you know? But one thing has been nagging me since this morning. About my meeting with Aydem."

"Sounds more like an ambush," Cillian murmured, his mustache fluttering with his breath.

"Oh, it definitely was. I didn't even get the chance to ask the guy all the questions I wanted to, you know? I had a shit-ton of grindylows to deal with, and obviously, I ran out of time."

The Clan leader chuckled, and Fiona covered her smile with the tips of her fingers.

"What I *don't* understand is why he would leave me there. He's the one who invited *me* to finally talk to him face to face. He's the one who kept sending me messages through his assistant about needing to dig into my own past to know what kinds of questions I should ask. So I dug. I found more questions. I asked them all, and he told me to pay attention and figure it out myself.

"I get that part. Nobody wants to explain all the answers to anyone. Fine. But I *know* he saw those grindylows coming for me. All he did was watch, back away, and disappear when I honestly thought… I mean, I thought I was gonna die. Is that crazy?"

"Not in the slightest," Fiona replied. "Ye *would* have if ye hadn't brought that bauble with ye."

"Yeah, well, it's been my only way out a few times now." Halsey turned the orb over in her hands, watching the metal that looked like smooth copper catch the firelight and wink in the room's semi-darkness.

"Ye're lucky ye thought ta craft it up the way ye did," Cillian added. "I'd trust a ball of magical sand over the Order o' Skrár ta save my life any day o' the week."

"Oh, is that right?" Halsey chuckled. "You're so confident just like that, huh?"

"Aye. Everyone who knows the Order of Skrár also knows they don't have the qualifications or the skillsets we do. Not the necessary ones that hold up in a full-on monster battle, anyhow. Would ye blame the man more if he was a normie walkin' by and happened ta see ya fight the things before scuttlin' off anyway?"

"No. You're right. The living records don't fight monsters. That's what *we're* here for."

"Bet he was right terrified out of his skin," Seamus cut in. "Couldn't handle a bit o' grindylow action and had ta bolt. Can't help it if it's in his nature, right?"

"Well, sure." She shot him a sidelong glance of mock exasperation. "If Halil Aydem were a *regular* human who didn't know what the hell he was seeing. But the Order of Skrár's supposed to know everything, remember? That's the whole reason I'd been trying so hard to have the damn meeting with him in the first place."

"Ye're not wrong, there, lass." After draining yet another glass of brandy, Cillian smacked his lips and stared across the room in contemplation. "The Order knows everythin' 'bout everyone, anyhow. This Aydem? I'd wager he would've known outright if ye couldn't handle all them grindylows on yer own. Better yet, he probably knew ye *could*. And *why*."

The large man raised his eyebrows and nodded slowly as if she knew what he was talking about.

She did.

Yeah, Aydem knows all about the copper orb and why I suddenly have a bunch of magic I shouldn't that works so well with the magic someone else left behind. That's why he wouldn't tell me a thing. He wants me to figure it out for myself. Not helpful. Not a very effective way to be a living record, either.

"Yeah, probably." Halsey sipped her sweet brandy and shrugged. "He could've checked up on me since then, though. A phone call or an email."

"Has he?" Seamus asked.

She pulled out her phone, which still had zero notifications for incoming anything, then opened her emails for a quick check. With a sigh, she stuffed her phone back in her pocket and shook her head. "Nothing."

"The fella likely figured ye'd worked it out on yer own, simple as that." Cillian leaned back and nodded in satisfaction as if they'd been sitting around to work out the problems of the universe and had succeeded.

"Or he thought the grindylows might kill me, and I'd disappear forever," Halsey countered. "One less stubborn thorn in his side. Whatever he *expected*, it's a shitty way to test someone's dedication to not dying."

Cillian found that particularly funny, and Halsey finally started to let it go. Or maybe all the whiskey and brandy had gone to her head enough to make her stop caring.

They stayed up later after that, among the rest of the Clan who'd survived the night so far and had given up on continuing to enjoy it. There was further conversation about how Halsey could figure out where her new magic had come from, what it meant both for her as an elemental and for the coming battle, and what her next steps should be.

The Havalons agreed they would pore through their own historical records about the varying types of magic passed down through generations of elementals. Plus, any and all records that might involve changing monsters or the Viking shipwreck in 953, or anything that might help arm them with as much information as possible.

"We'll ask the Clan elders too," Fiona assured her after the dwindling group of revelers had offered their suggestions and comments. "I can't promise ye anythin' from them, mind, but there's a small chance they're still sharp enough ta recall *somethin'* useful."

"She means *she'll* ask the elders," Cillian amended with a laugh. "My great-granda can't stand the sight o' me or any of my siblin's. But my lovely wife, here? Why, she's the only one our forefathers even care ta *see*, let alone converse with or help in any way—"

"Oh, shush." Fiona smacked his arm, which only made him laugh louder. "It's the shite like *that* comin' out yer mouth that made 'em tired of listenin' to ya."

"Aye. Just so." The large man stopped chuckling long enough to pull a straight face at his wife. "Ye're right, dear. 'Tis the *only* thing they can't stand 'bout me, seein' as ye're no prettier than I am…"

Seamus' mother rolled her eyes and ignored her husband's jokes, then took Halsey's hands. "Thank ye fer sharin' yerself with us tonight, Halsey. I do hope it's not the last time, though I'm sure I can speak fer all of us when I say 'twould be better under different circumstances."

"Took the words right out of my mouth." Halsey squeezed the woman's hands in reply.

"Ye're welcome ta any room ye like in the big house."

Fiona nodded toward her husband. "It's time I put this giant, matted lug ta bed. And I'll add one more ta the breakfast table in the mornin', aye?"

"I sure hope I'm still here in the morning. So yes. Please. And thank you."

"Oh! Listen to ye. So polite 'n gracious 'bout every little thing." The woman sent a pointed look at her son first, then directly at her husband while Cillian sniggered and spread his arms.

"What did I do now?"

"Maybe it's not 'bout what ye've *already* done, eh? Did ye ever think o' that?"

"Oh, so ye can read the *future* now. Is that it, woman?"

"Aye, and believe ye me, boyo, ye don't want me repeatin' it."

"Are ye *certain*?"

Rolling her eyes and shaking her head, Fiona guided her husband across the center of the big house toward the massive staircase. She occasionally shoved him to one side or the other when it looked like he was shuffling too close to a wall, or a corner, or the furniture.

Halsey and Seamus watched until the older couple had disappeared up the stairs, then they burst out laughing.

"Are they gonna be okay up there all by themselves?"

"Well, *I'm* certainly not goin' after 'em just ta be sure. Are ye?"

She fervently shook her head, still trying to catch her breath after laughing so hard.

But he did show her to what served as her room for the duration of her stay at the Havalon Clan's big house.

He stayed with her a little longer afterward.

Halsey hadn't known she'd needed a night like tonight so badly until she found herself on the verge of sleep, warm and safe and surprisingly happy despite everything she knew was coming in the future.

She figured she'd earned this much.

CHAPTER TWENTY-THREE

Halsey stayed in Ireland with the Havalons for the next four days. It wasn't quite the vacation she'd been trying to give herself before her entire world of monster hunting and family politics imploded, but it was much needed and far more than worth it.

Seamus showed her around all his favorite places out in the country, and they took the opportunity to spend as much time with each other as possible while they had the chance. There was no telling what might pop up for all of them over the next several months, though there had been a mostly unspoken consensus that all the elemental Clans were about to see massive changes. Most of them for the worse.

Even with that knowledge looming over their heads, the young elementals managed to enjoy getting to know each other *without* turning to doom-and-gloom talk. Instead, they focused on each other, their pasts, a few monster-hunting stories worth telling, and whatever else they could think of to pass the time, stay in the present, and leave the future far ahead of them where it belonged.

Halsey could have gotten used to having a joyous, boisterous, graciously welcoming family around her to cook her meals, offer her whatever she might need, and throw Clan celebrations every night. But on that fourth day in Ireland, she knew it was time to go home.

Brigham still hadn't tried to reach her, which made her grateful and concerned in equal parts. The Ambrosius Council hadn't decided to serve her up any other last-minute missions, fortunately, so she hadn't heard from them, either. And, of course, there was still no correspondence from Halil Aydem.

Halsey was convinced the man she'd met from the Order of Skrár had expected there would be no need to contact her in the future. The more she thought about her harrowing morning with him, the way he'd reacted, what he'd said, and how he'd left her in the middle of a deadly grindylow ambush to fend for herself, the more convinced she became that the whole thing had been a test. While Aydem had given her an opportunity to "prove herself," whatever he'd meant by that, he hadn't actually expected her to pass.

When she told the Havalons she'd bought her last-minute international flight back to the States and would be leaving early the next morning, her hosts put together another elaborate sendoff for her. This time, they didn't say their goodbyes with the kind of heartfelt gesture they'd made the last time. No elaborate necklace embellished with the teeth and claws of the silverback alpha she'd killed. No formal declaration of gratitude and friendship.

No sticking her with a new name like Alpha Hunter, which might have been starting to grow on her.

Instead, she was hugged by more Havalons than she'd realized existed and lived in the big house, sent off with snacks for the drive back to the airport, and thanked for everything she'd done, experienced, and shared with their Clan.

Fiona handed her a small black notebook with only the first few pages penciled in. "If ye need ta reach out ta any one of us faster'n the usual way, call these numbers. Emails, too. We'll keep workin' on puttin' together a runnin' list of resources and whatever we manage ta find on what we're facin'. With all of us on board, hopefully, we can solve this brain-buster of a puzzle before the time fer it runs out."

"Thank you." Halsey hugged the woman warmly, pocketed the tiny notebook, and turned to Cillian.

"Emergency messagin' system, too," the giant man added as he pointed at the pocket where she'd stuffed the notebook. "Yer account and all the information's already been set up fer ye, lass. Keep it on. Keep it close. We're not the kinda folks ta worry 'bout every little thing that might be headin' our way, but we *do* know how ta prepare for it when need be. And share it with those o' the Ambrosius Clan more likely not ta toss it out the window than use it, aye?"

"Good thing I've already got a few people in mind." She reached out to clasp the Clan leader's hand, but he jerked her forward and wrapped her in an enormous bear hug instead, laughing all the while.

Then Halsey and Seamus piled into the Volkswagen

and took off across the Irish countryside, this time headed for Dublin International.

Their drive was almost entirely silent. She didn't have another episode requiring a stop in the middle of nowhere so she could breathe again, and he didn't babble amicably along about his relatives in an attempt to ease her mind. Their last four days together weren't as long as either of them would have liked, but it was enough for now.

At the airport, Seamus parked at the curb in front of the entrance for departing flights. He hauled Halsey's bag from the car and dropped it on the sidewalk before wrapping her up in his arms and kissing her like they were back at the Havalons' big house instead of saying their goodbyes out in public.

When he finally released her, Halsey couldn't help but laugh as she looked into his glimmering blue eyes. "Don't tell me that was in case you never see me again."

"O' course not." He tucked her dark hair behind her ear, then held her by the waist with both hands and grins. "It's 'cause I know I will. Just try not ta make it as long as the last time, aye?"

"You mean go find these mystery beasts and the Mother of Monsters as soon as I possibly can? Well, it's a good thing I've got *you* to convince me of that. I was actually thinking about sitting back and taking my own sweet time."

"Aye, I bet ye were. Sounds like somethin' ye'd do." Seamus kissed her again, which was much shorter and sweeter this time, then grabbed her bag and valiantly helped her haul the strap over one shoulder. "Ye take care o' yerself, Hal. And maybe give me a ring every now 'n then, eh?"

"Yeah, you too."

They turned back to look at each other more than once as she headed into the airport, and he went back to the car. But Halsey didn't go inside until she watched the good-looking, mischievous, astoundingly insightful Irishman pull away from the curb and disappear into the lines of cars pulling up to drop off departing friends and family.

The only thing that dampened the sendoff was the feeling that struck Halsey the second before she stepped into the airport terminal.

Like she was being watched again. Followed. Studied.

She paused in front of the automatic doors when she recognized the feeling, which hadn't hit her since pulling up at the Irish pub with Seamus the day she'd arrived.

More grindylows or something else?

Her instant gut response would have been to turn and frantically search the constantly moving waves of cars and people coming in and out of the airport around her.

Yet during the last five days in the open countryside of the Emerald Isle, as much of a voluntary time off and whole-body restart as she was likely to get in the foreseeable future, Halsey had learned quite a bit about what her gut response had been telling her for most of her life.

While her monster-hunting instincts were honed to a fine point and had rarely steered her wrong, a massive percentage of her reactions, thought processes, and day-to-day decisions had been manufactured by the monster-hunting militia she served, the Ambrosius Clan Council, and the members of her family she'd trusted the most.

Everyone but Brigham had let her down in one way or another. And while she'd had nothing to do with the lies and secrets her family had been keeping from her, she also knew now that none of it was her fault.

None of it had inherently been her responsibility to fix, either, but that *was* something she could take into her own hands and had during her time in Ireland.

So she stood in front of the airport doors, rolled her shoulders back, lifted her chin, and let the sensation of being watched wash over her before making her decision.

Fuck it. If the little shit that's been watching me wants to make a move, fine. It's gonna take a lot more than making me feel like I'm being spied on to stop me now.

She stepped into the building and refused to give it any more thought as she started the long trip back to the home part of her truly had missed since she and Brigham had taken off on their poorly briefed barghest mission.

Another part of her had wanted to leave her family in Texas behind her forever. That part would have to wait until the elementals finished what needed to be done. Together.

CHAPTER TWENTY-FOUR

With nothing to do but wait for the airline to get her where she needed to go before waiting some more to land and make her connecting flight, Halsey decided to prepare as much as she possibly could *before* getting back home. It was tempting to send out a giant group email to all the Ambrosius cousins of her generation about everything that had happened. And maybe even a group text to go with it, simply to get their attention.

No less than ten of their cousins around the same age would be on board with the broad plan she'd made with the Havalons and Grendiers during her visit. She knew that without a doubt. Even Jasper was likely to hop aboard the Reunite-the-Elemental-Clans train and join them, though she was pretty sure he had a wife and kids he might be more hesitant to leave behind.

Greta, of course, was also on that list. The woman had made a show of being perfectly content to live out the rest of her days in her cozy-but-chaotic bungalow along the river, agreeing peaceably with her own family's decision to banish her. However, Halsey had a feeling that was only for show.

Her grandmother had told her everything she'd known, the whole truth, even the parts that had planted a small seed of resentment in her granddaughter for having kept these family secrets for so long. The woman had also seemed to place the mantel of responsibility and action onto Halsey's shoulders, giving her enough information to stoke her curiosity and interest but leaving the rest up to the next generation.

Yet Halsey was convinced that, given the opportunity, her Meemaw would jump right back into action the moment it was called for. Like the others willing to put their differences aside for their common goal. Greta Ambrosius was still a force to be reckoned with.

When Halsey took the time to think about it, she gave her father an eighty-percent chance of standing with her and the younger Ambrosius generation to do what was right. Even if it meant turning away from the siblings and cousins he'd conspired with to kick Greta off the Council and out of their lives. Or so they'd thought.

He came to my house, apologized to me, and said he was behind me all the way. When the time comes, Dad'll follow his conscience. He's got too much to lose.

Before she could bring herself to write up an email that would preemptively prepare the majority of active Ambrosius militia operatives, she had to get in touch with Brigham.

She'd sent him a text while waiting to board her first flight out of Dublin.

Getting on a flight home soon. Be back on the estate probably by 7 p.m. We have a lot to talk about.

Only after she'd boarded the plane and settled into her window seat did she get a reply, which was nothing more than a thumbs-up emoji.

Great. He's still pissed and weirded out by everything. I need to try to make this right before I get back home and in his face.

She typed up another quick message she hoped would go through before takeoff and lack of cell service.

I'm sorry I didn't come home with you after Coningsby. I really needed this time, and I feel like I finally got my head screwed on straight again. Let me make it up to you? I'll grab a case of Monster Bash on the way to your place...

Then she had to wait the whole nine hours and thirty minutes of her nonstop flight from Dublin to Dallas, which she'd been extremely fortunate to snag with such late notice. Waiting that long to see what her cousin's response might have been was agonizing, to say the least. But her phone buzzed in her pocket a minute before the aircraft touched down on the tarmac, and her heart fluttered in her chest.

This time, Brigham had sent her *two* thumbs-up emojis and zero words.

"Oh, come on. Seriously?"

The woman in the seat beside her gave Halsey a quick double-take with what looked like a disturbed frown.

Halsey chuckled and wiggled her phone at the woman. "Family. Gotta love coming home, right?"

The woman didn't say anything while she unfastened her seatbelt and tightened her hold on the purse in her lap with both hands.

With no checked bags and no one to wait for, Halsey moved through the airport as quickly as possible. It was a minor relief not to feel the sensation of being watched in the Dallas airport. It would have been vastly naïve of her to think the grindylows who shared their strange hive-mind communication didn't also exist in the U.S., but dealing with tiny bug-eyed spies with sharp teeth and clawed webbed feet wasn't anywhere close to the top of her priority list right now.

She checked her phone again while waiting in line for a rental car to get her back out to Lufkin. Nothing.

Then waiting became too much for her to bear, and she called her cousin directly.

The line rang three times, and she almost thought he wouldn't answer simply to spite her longer. Finally, Brigham picked up.

"What?"

Halsey snorted. "Hey to you too."

"I'm kinda busy right now, so... What's up?"

Kinda busy? Damn, he's super pissed.

She drew a deep breath and tried not to let her annoyance or trepidation show too much in her voice. "Just thought it was weird that you're only texting me emojis. Wanted to make sure everything's okay."

"You're freaking out about emojis? Come on. Everyone

uses emojis. It's the new text. Listen, I'm—Jesus Christ, Owen. Are you *serious* right now?"

A low murmur came over the line in the background, but Halsey couldn't make out the words.

"No. Come on. You've been hauling that shit around with you every single day since...I don't even wanna know how long. Everywhere. You're not twelve anymore, dude. Put it away."

Another pause for the point their cousin Owen was obviously trying to argue, then Brigham sighed heavily. "I don't wanna see it anymore, okay? Makes me feel like I'm living in some kinda alternate universe of our lives, and those are already fucked up enough right now."

Definitely in a bad mood. Seriously, I was only gone for four days after he flew home. How much could go wrong?

She waited for her cousin to quit bickering with Owen, then Brigham's voice was suddenly loud and up close again.

"If you're calling for someone to pick you up, I can't. Sorry. I'm busy working on some stuff right now, and—"

"I don't need you to pick me up, Brigham. I'm getting a rental." Halsey paused to lean sideways and check how many other people were ahead of her at the counter. The line had hardly moved. "But thanks anyway."

Her cousin snorted, then there was another brief pause that felt unnatural for the kind of relationship they had. Which, judging by the way he'd been avoiding her and obviously didn't want to talk, might be in the process of changing. "So what do you want, Halsey?" he finally asked.

Halsey, huh? The red flags keep piling up.

"Well, first," she started. "I wanted to let you know I'm back in Texas."

"Yeah, I got your texts. Hence the emojis."

She rolled her eyes and forced herself not to be a smartass with her reply, which had a high potential to push him over the edge. "And I wanted to make sure you're okay. You know, 'cause we haven't talked since—"

"Dude, you need to make up your mind about this kinda thing." At first, she thought he was talking to Owen, but then he kept going. "First, you wanna ship me home by myself after a sour mission that almost made me permanently...I don't know. Undead, or whatever. Just so you could go have your fun little private fling with a handsome Havalon. Which I get. Totally understandable. So I left you alone. Now you're blowing up my phone because we haven't talked in four days, and you're worried about me? Come on, Halsey. You can't have both whenever you feel like it only because...you feel like it."

She blinked quickly, his words sinking in with crystal clarity because she knew he was right. She had a lot to make up for, starting right now with not taking no for an answer. "So you'd rather I not tell you I'm home and not tell you about everything that's happened since Coningsby?"

"Honestly, yeah. I'd rather you didn't." Brigham chuckled, but it was bitter and tight, and it fell flat compared to his usual fun, easygoing attitude. "And no, I don't need to know about everything you and Seamus did while you were frolicking through fields of clover together or some shit. I only hope it was worth it. That's about all I—"

"Brigham, it wasn't a detour to go...*frolicking* with

Seamus. Jesus, that makes us sound like a couple of sheep." It was supposed to be a joke, but she didn't get so much as a snigger out of her cousin. She inhaled and exhaled slowly. "Listen, Brigham. I know you're pissed at me right now—"

"Oh, you *do*? Congratulations."

"—but I need to talk to you. Badly. In person. As soon as I get back to Lufkin. You need to know about everything that happened after you left England, and I need to tell you. So can I please come over with beer, so I can fill you in on everything you missed? It's important stuff, man."

"Huh. Everything I missed..." Brigham clicked his tongue a few times, then grunted and shouted away from the phone, "Dude, did everything I said go one ear and out the other? No, you can't do that there. That's where I eat!" He sighed heavily and sounded like he was about to explode when he finally spoke to Halsey again. "Listen, now's not a good time."

"Well, it'll still take me three hours after I finally get a rental."

"Yeah, *today's* not a good time. Maybe the rest of the week, too. I don't know. Just...go home and do your thing, okay? I'll do mine. We'll wait for another mission assignment and figure it out from there."

"Brigham, come on. If you give me an hour, I can—"

"Drive safe."

The line went dead, and Halsey stared at the home screen of her phone in disbelief.

The person at the front of the car-rental line *finally* moved away from the counter with their new temporary set of keys, and everyone in line took one small step forward.

Fine. If he wants to play it that way, I'll play. He called me out on my bullshit once upon a time. Only fair that I return the favor. And it's only because I love you, cuz.

She used the rest of her obnoxiously long wait in line to draft the email on her phone that she didn't think she'd be sending until after she and Brigham sat down to hash everything out first.

He'd left her no choice. Though the immediate danger wasn't right on top of them like it was during a mission, or even when Halsey and Brigham had gone off to find without knowing what to expect, she was still certain of one important fact.

They were running out of time.

She got the email sent before she'd even received her rental car at the airport. And for the entire three-hour drive back home, her phone exploded with text replies from every one of her cousins she'd reached out to. All of them were coming. All of them would be there. All of them were willing to help out in whatever way they could. Which was great because Halsey would need some backup if she intended to do this today.

Brigham wouldn't be happy.

At slightly before 7:00 p.m., she parked in the lot of her cousin's apartment complex and hauled the two cases of Monster Bash ale she'd bought from the back seat. Then she hurried across the lot and up to the apartment she'd only stepped inside a handful of times. Halsey preferred to stay at her cottage nestled in the woods when she wasn't on duty and out on active missions, but this wasn't one of those times.

She had to set down one of the cases so she could knock on Brigham's door. Despite being able to hear him grumbling inside at someone, presumably still Owen, he took his sweet time answering the door. So she knocked again.

"Okay, okay. I'm coming! Hold on!" Stomping footsteps headed her way, then the door whipped open. Brigham blinked in surprise, scrutinized her, then sighed. "Nope."

He tried to swing the door shut in her face, but Halsey shoved the other case of beer in the doorjamb to stop him, aided by her boot against the door. "Hear me out."

"Not interested. I told you to go home."

"Brigham, I'm not gonna let you *hide* from me until something terrible happens, and you come crawling out of your cave—"

"Well, you *should*. It's what I want. I know it's not really your style to *think* about what I might want, so now I'm telling you. Glad you're home. Awesome. I'm not in a great mood for visitors right now. Bye."

He tried to close the door again, but she kept a firm enough grip on it to make that impossible. Plus, she hadn't moved the case of beer.

When he realized he was getting nowhere, Brigham heaved a massive sigh and refused to look at her. "What do you want, Halsey?"

"To talk." She nodded toward the Monster Bash. "To have a few cold ones because I know this is your favorite. To apologize. And to tell you *everything*. Because you deserve to know, and we have a *lot* of work ahead of us if, you know, you're remotely interested in living past the end of the year, probably. So what do you say?"

Brigham glared at her and tilted his head. "The end of the year, huh?"

"It's a conservative guess."

"Whoa, is that Halsey standing out there?" Owen called from the living room. "Hey, Halsey! Come on in!"

"Thanks." She muscled her way past Brigham, leaving the second case of beer in front of his door in case he wanted to bring it inside and restock his supply. She knew he would.

"Okay, no." With the door still open, he spun toward his cousins and pointed at Owen. "You don't live here, man. You don't get to invite in anyone you want—"

"Want a beer?" Halsey hefted the case onto the kitchen table with a *thump*.

"Monster Bash? Hell yeah, I do." Owen rose from his seat to join her for a cold bottle, and they both ignored Brigham's sullen protests.

With another sigh, he started to close the door, then eyed the second case on the stoop. He rolled his eyes and grabbed the case before practically slamming the door shut.

While his cousins chatted away, Brigham skulked around his apartment, refusing to take a beer from Halsey and choosing to grab one for himself instead. After ten minutes, he'd finally had enough and whirled on her to shout, "Why the hell are you *here*?"

"Because it's important." Halsey sipped her beer and smiled. "Remember that one time you almost got your head chopped off with one of my throwing axes 'cause you walked into *my* house unannounced and uninvited?"

His only reply was to glare at her.

She shrugged. "That's what I'm doing. Same thing."

"No, it's not—"

"You're self-destructing 'cause you're pissed at me, Brigham. And I get it. You have every right to be. But I have a *lot* of new puzzle pieces. They all fit together, and I'm gonna need your help to put them together the right way. So please sit down, stop yelling at me, and hear me out, huh?"

For a moment, he looked like he would try to throw her out again. Then he angrily glugged more beer and noisily scooted one of the kitchen chairs from beneath the table. When he plopped into it, he scowled at the colorfully illustrated cards scattered on the table in front of Owen. "And dude. I told you to clean this shit up, man. I don't play board games."

"It's Fire and Realm, bro." Owen shot him a dirty look, but he quickly collected the cards and handbooks he'd laid out before muttering, "Not a card game."

Brigham glared at Halsey, slumping in his chair with the full attitude of a moody teenager. "Well?"

She pulled out her phone to check the time. "Just a little longer."

"You said you're here to talk, Halsey. So talk. I don't get why you'd have to wait for anything else to happen before—"

Another brisk knock came at the front door.

Growling in frustration, Brigham leapt from his chair

and stormed across the apartment again. "This is ridiculous."

When he opened the door and started to tell whoever it was to go away, he wasn't buying, the smiling faces of Cadence and Charlie greeted him.

"Heya, Brigham! We made it!"

"What the hell?" Brigham was forced aside as two more of his cousins traipsed through the door.

"Brought some fried chicken," Cadence announced as she lifted two cardboard to-go boxes with a third under her arm. "Should be enough."

"Three family-sized boxes?" Charlie snorted. "It better be."

Brigham stared after them in shock and slowly pushed the front door shut before it blasted open again without warning.

"We're here!" Nick shouted as he waltzed into the apartment. "And lemme tell ya, if you're lookin' for cookies, don't go to the stupid bakery in town. They charge *way* too much."

"Where did those come from?" Aldous asked as he followed his cousin inside.

"Grocery store, baby. Got 'em on discount, too."

"Sweet."

"What the fuck?" Brigham whispered, his eyes wide in disbelief. Nobody bothered to tell him what was happening. Instead, everyone focused on setting up a makeshift buffet along the edge of his kitchen counter.

"Hey, Brigham. You got anything to put the paper plates on?"

"Of course he doesn't. Just stick 'em on the counter. It's clean. Probably. Hey, you *do* clean your counters, right?"

"Hand me one of those beers, bro."

"Need a hand with that one too?"

"Who's got the plastic forks and shit?"

Over the next ten minutes, four more of Halsey and Brigham's cousins, those who'd been at the surprise party she'd thrown for him after he'd been released from the medical ward, showed up to join the potluck turned emergency meeting Halsey had called. All before she'd left the Dallas airport.

When the last of them walked inside, the door was promptly locked and shut. The feast spread out on the counter was complete with potato salad, green beans, and cornbread.

Brigham grabbed his shaggy auburn hair with both hands and stared blankly at the whole thing. "I don't get it…"

"Grab a plate and eat, cuz." Halsey clapped a hand on his shoulder and nodded. "Then I'll explain everything."

After everyone had a drink in hand and a full plate in front of them, that was exactly what she did.

Halsey told her cousins absolutely everything from beginning to end. She didn't leave anything out, including the fact that their own Council had started taking paying jobs from unvetted clients, the incredibly personal lie about her mom's death, and how the rest of their family had failed to deal with it in a productive way. As well as the lengths the Council was willing to go to when they'd banned Greta from the estate house.

She even made it a point to tell Brigham directly, in front of everyone, that she'd kept some small secrets. Like trying to meet with Halil Aydem and succeeding before being interrupted by a grindylow swarm. She admitted that she'd made a massive mistake in not telling him everything from the start. That he had every right to be pissed, and that she was trying to make things right.

That made him particularly uncomfortable, but he didn't blow up at her in front of all these cousins.

Which was exactly the way Halsey had planned it.

After she finished telling a large chunk of her family about everything that had been going on behind the scenes and under all their noses, she told them about the Council meeting at the Havalon estate. She made it perfectly clear that the Grendier siblings who'd been there had represented their entire Clan and were more than willing to work with all elementals to track down these mystery monsters. And, of course, to eventually stand against the mother of them all, the Blood Matriarch, when the time came.

When she finished without being interrupted once, Halsey felt surprisingly empty. Then she realized it wasn't so much emptiness as it was the feeling of being free—from the lies, from the sneaking around, from living under the shadow of their ancestors' choices. And it felt amazing.

"So," she finished after tossing back the rest of her third beer. "That's everything, and I do mean *everything*. I wanted you all to be here so everybody could get the same information at once. And to get everyone's take on this. Because

I'm sure you've all figured out by now that the Council isn't gonna drop everything to help the other Clans because of anything *I* tell them. And I was the only one there. But if *we* decide to start working on this now, if we decide to start doing things the right way from here on out, we can do some crazy-awesome shit together. I only know I can't do it alone."

She met Brigham's gaze as she finished her final statement and spread her arms. "So, what d'ya say, cuz?"

Brigham stared at her, then puffed a sigh and shrugged. "I say you're fucking insane, Hal. But we already know that, so... Why the hell not?"

As their other cousins nodded and murmured their agreement, ready to step forward and take a stand, Halsey grinned. "I knew you'd say that."

CHAPTER TWENTY-FIVE

The dozen Ambrosius cousins unofficially made Brigham's apartment their base of operations, mostly because it wasn't located on the family estate, so they didn't run the risk of being intercepted by anyone on the Council who might try to stop them.

With the exception of Halsey, who was still banned from the Clan Library, they checked out as many tomes, scrolls, historical records, and personal accounts as possible to pore through anything and everything that might be related to the weird new creatures the Grendiers had discovered. Everyone agreed that Halsey's theory about these monsters being from *before* the great war was the best information they had to go on, and the extent of their resources only went so far as what was in the Ambrosius Library.

That didn't discourage them from trying literally everything.

After a few weeks, Jasper finally accepted the constantly repeated invitation to join them. They filled him in on everything he'd missed before receiving his unexpectedly enthusiastic response. Of course he was in.

For once, Halsey didn't have to be the one to explain everything to everyone.

They decided together not to go to anyone on the Council about what they were doing, thinking it was best to wait until they had the proof they were looking for. It seemed Halsey's curiosity and her tendency to shirk some of the militia's rules had thoroughly rubbed off on the rest of her generation, and it served them incredibly well.

At first, the realization that she'd finally found belonging within her family made her uncomfortable. She'd always had Brigham, of course, and Greta. Now, she was surrounded by other Ambrosius monster hunters she'd grown up with, lived with, and served with all her life. They were adults. They were skilled, with the knowledge and experience required to do what Ambrosius monster hunters had always been doing. And they were aware enough of the situation to understand that sitting on the sidelines and waiting for the Council to come to its senses wasn't a viable option anymore.

If she'd known so many of her cousins and extended cousins had felt the same way she did but hadn't found the one thing to push them into action, Halsey would have conscripted their help a long time ago. Better late than never, though.

They hadn't mentioned any of their endeavors to Greta or Aiden yet. Halsey assured everyone that those two, at the least, were also on their side and would follow them when they had an actionable plan. Until then, it would cause too much friction among the Clan, especially when

Aiden still held a Council seat. As soon as they found what they were looking for, or the emergency-messaging system set up between all three elemental Clans sounded the alarm that the Havalons or Grendiers had found something, Greta and Aiden would be let in on the secret.

It only took about a week before the group of young Ambrosius elementals together started calling themselves the A-Team. And it stuck.

Brigham was admittedly resentful of the fact that it took fourteen Ambrosiuses to finally decide that the name fit, but he recovered quickly and took to calling the group by this name every chance he got. Apparently, that was all he needed to rub it in Halsey's face and remind her that she'd always shot down "A-Team" as a codename for the two of them.

Not everyone could meet at Brigham's apartment every day because the Council still assigned active missions. There were always monsters to hunt. Still, they returned to his apartment after finishing each of those missions. Those left behind continued the work until others could pick up the slack.

The work was slow and painstaking, but with everyone pitching in, there was plenty of beer and coffee to keep them going through the night. Sometimes both. Everyone helped with food, taking turns grocery shopping to stock up Brigham's kitchen for however many days it would hold food for fourteen people.

Halsey would never have imagined she would come home from the worst discovery of her life—her ability to *control* monsters instead of fighting them or killing them—to find the majority of active Ambrosius operatives on her side and willing to help her in the fight. No, they didn't have an enormous estate in the middle of a field by the mountains, and they didn't bring the whole family together night after night to celebrate the joys of being, but she started to feel like she was part of a family again.

This time, that family shared her lineage, her last name, and the history that had partially gotten them into this mess.

And none of it had come from the Council.

It was a silver lining around the grueling work of searching through everything the Ambrosius Clan possessed to find *something* to lead them in the right direction. But it was worth it.

The answer they'd all spent weeks searching for finally came in the most unexpected way imaginable.

The A-Team had spent the last five hours strewn around Brigham's apartment, sorting through the records they'd already looked over and those they hadn't, grabbing new ones from the unread pile, picking a comfortable seat with a drink in hand or a freshly made sandwich. Gentle music played in the background, and it felt like any other day since they'd started this process.

Halsey finished reading an old, mind-numbingly boring book about the history of Ambrosius elementals' names and where they'd come from, then finally had to stretch her legs.

"I'm gonna get a drink," she told Brigham, sitting on the floor beside her. "You want anything?"

"Yeah, if there's orange juice left in the fridge. Thanks." He didn't even look up from his reading, but she didn't mind.

No one looked up as Halsey crossed the living room and headed into the kitchen. After pouring a glass of orange juice for Brigham and cracking open a bottle of mineral water for herself, Halsey took a few giant swigs, sighed, then prepared to get back to work.

On the way, she passed Brigham's kitchen table, which had become the "book area" where all read and unread documents were held in an attempt to keep the rest of the apartment as tidy as possible. Owen sat alone at the end of the table, where he'd cleared off a small patch of the table, with his head bent low over the workspace.

Colorful cards were laid out in rows in front of him, illustrated with images of fantastical creatures, tools, and lights. She didn't understand any of it, but one of the cards caught her eye.

Halsey stopped beside the table and tried to be casual about it when she asked, "What are you doing?"

"What?" Owen looked up at her with wide eyes, like he'd been caught with his hand in the cookie jar. "Just a thing. I'm taking a break. Everyone's gotta take breaks sometimes."

"Hey, I get it. If you need a break, no problem. I'm only wondering what you're up to."

Owen's instant fear faded, and he smirked before looking back down at his card. "Fire and Realm."

"What's that?"

"Are you fucking *kidding* me right now?" Brigham groaned from his spot on the floor. Several of their cousins looked up from their diligent work, interrupted by the loud shouting and Brigham's obvious exasperation. "Man, I told you not to bring those here. *Especially* when everyone else is trying to work. And you keep bringing a *game*?"

"It's not just a game," Owen replied defensively. "It's a community."

"Oh, yeah. Right. Awesome." Brigham rolled his eyes and set aside the tome he'd been reading before pointing at the one Ambrosius cousin everyone knew had always been slow on the draw. "Right now, dude, you're in *our* community. A real one. So put your little trading cards away and find something else to do on your break. I'm so *tired* of seeing those things all over my apartment!"

A few chuckles moved around the room, the other cousins laughing at Brigham's words, the fact that he was so upset, or the fact that one of their own had a love for Fire and Realm when that was already practically their life anyway.

Owen glared at him, then sighed and began to slowly pack up his things.

"Hold on a sec," Halsey interrupted, holding out a hand to stop him. "What are these for?"

"The cards?" Owen shrugged. "They're to add to the gameplay. The whole thing revolves around rolling dice, right? You play with other people on a team and go through the whole world or a storyline or a campaign, whatever you want. Most of the world's been set up already, but it leaves a surprising amount of room for coming up with your own stuff if that's what you're into."

"Did you come up with these?"

"The cards?" He snorted. "No. They come in a premade

set. These are creature cards. They came from a past version of the game called—"

"She doesn't *care* about all the details, man." Brigham dragged his hands down the sides of his face and groaned again. "Give it a rest."

"Hey, did she ask you?" Owen snapped. "No. She's asking *me*. And as far as I know, you're the only person here who gives a shit about me taking my breaks with a fun thing *I* like to do, so maybe you should shut up and mind your own business. How does *that* sound?"

The apartment fell silent as the rest of the A-Team watched the argument, all of them surprised by the fact that Owen was standing up for anything. Especially against Brigham.

Brigham was equally surprised. He stared at his cousin, blinked a few times, then snorted and shrugged. "Whatever, man. I'm telling you right now, she's not sitting down to play that shit with you. Ever. And we still have a shit-ton of books to read through."

Then he returned to his reading, scoffing and shaking his head. No one else said anything, but a multitude of surprised looks were shared around the room.

Halsey cleared her throat and leaned toward Owen. "I am interested in *one* detail, actually," she told him gently.

"Sure." He shrugged without looking at her but stopped picking up the cards. "What do you wanna know?"

"What's this?" She pointed at a card with an illustration of a grotesque humanoid figure. Long limbs, a gangly stature, the whole thing painted in dark brown and black with nasty-looking spikes sticking up all over its body. The background was only a swirl of gray and black, but the figure in the forefront cast an impressive image.

The reason it had caught her attention was that it was startlingly close to the image she'd crafted in her mind from Alvara and Dietrich's description of the mystery monster they'd been trying to track down.

No such thing as coincidence, right? So prove it.

"This one?" Owen's smile returned as he pointed at the card. "That's one of the Crimen."

"Okay." She nodded, waiting for him to continue before realizing she would have to prompt him. "What does it do?"

"Why are you suddenly so interested?"

"I don't know, man. You've been playing this game or whatever for so long. There must be something about it. You know, seeing as we go on quests and fight monsters in real life and everything."

"Yeah, but we don't get to choose any of that shit, do we?" His smile faded a little, then he tapped the card in question. "Right. Crimen. This one's actually one of my favorites 'cause they're so nuts. Hell of a monster to go up against in a campaign. They can literally be anything, depending on what you want—"

"Just the monster, Owen." Halsey plastered on a gentle smile and nodded. "Not the rest of the game. Pretend it's a monster you're about to go up against in real life, right? On a mission. *That* kinda summary."

"Give me a break," Brigham muttered before angrily flipping another page in his tome without caring about whatever damage he might do to the old family document.

"Right." Owen studied the card for another moment,

then cleared his throat. "The Crimen. They're tortured creatures from the Far Realm, right? Meaning not the Prime Material Plane. Used to be living beings, but they entered the Far Realm, where corporeal forms and time and space don't exist the same way. I guess you could say it kinda mutated them."

"Uh-huh..."

"After that, all they wanted was to get *back* to the Prime Material Plane. Their home. But creatures from the Far Realm can't exist *there*, either. It's not a two-way street. Anyway, the Crimen's main goal is to come back to the Material Plane and taint it enough to be like the Far Realm so they can exist in their true forms instead of always having to protect themselves.

"See, their mutated bodies can't handle the Material Plane. And the part of them that's all Far Realm? Well, it allows them to make this kind of armor around themselves that they have to wear all the time only to exist in the realm they used to call home. It's called Crimen Rosin, right? *Super* strong. Almost impenetrable. They wear it on them all the time because that's how they survive. Plus, they use it to build their little hive things where more of them can live together. They don't have to wear their living-armor rosin inside one of those things because it's made to be more like the Far Realm—"

"More monster abilities, Owen," Halsey interrupted, her heart pounding in her chest. "Less lore."

"Gotcha, gotcha. Um... So the Crimen don't really like to fight that much. They're more interested in tainting the Material Plane so it's more comfortable for *them*. And they'll try to turn other creatures into something *like* them.

People become more Crimen. The animals, though… If they lock their jaws on an animal for eight hours, it blights the creature. Then you've got a nasty Far-Realm critter running around and serving the Crimen.

"But if they can avoid conflict altogether, they will. They're super-fast, hard to injure 'cause of the rosin armor, and in some instances, they can even disappear to confuse their enemies. Only for short periods of time, though. What they're insanely good at is subterfuge. Camouflage. The real high-level ones can change their appearances to look like anyone they want. The goal is to infiltrate their enemy, sow deceit, lies, and misdirection, and weaken their opponent from within. So, spies from the Far Realm try to turn the Material Plane inside-out by basically being sneaky. They're more prone to chipping off their armor and hurting themselves than actually winning a battle.

"Oh! And whenever players see a whole bunch of Crimen suddenly appearing, it's because they're heralding the arrival of some *super*-intense, high-level bad guy from the Far Realm. Could be a bigger, badder Crimen. Could be something else. You never know. So…yeah. That's the general summary, I guess."

He grinned proudly, studying her face to gauge her reaction. "Anything else you wanna know?"

Halsey couldn't stop staring at the card.

Was there anything else she wanted to *know*?

Holy shit. It's been right here in front of us the whole time. How the hell is that even possible?

The apartment had fallen silent now, which Owen didn't seem to realize while he waited for Halsey's response. "Everything okay?"

From his place on the floor, Brigham dropped the tome he was reading with a loud *thump*. His jaw dropped open, and he stared at his cousins hovering over the illustrated pieces of a fantasy role-playing game.

"Holy shit," Cadence called from where she sat cross-legged on the couch at the far end of the apartment. "It's a Crimen."

"Yeah, that's what I said." Owen started to laugh at her but realized the rest of the A-Team was staring at him in disbelief. "What? Did I say something?"

"I'm pretty sure you just said everything, Owen." Halsey clapped a hand on his shoulder and grinned.

"No." Brigham furiously shook his head. "No fucking way."

"I don't know how it's possible, but this is it. Hidden elemental knowledge of the *real* world sitting right here in front of us, cuz." She gestured at the card on the table. "In *color*, even."

"Uh-uh. No." He leapt to his feet, stormed toward them, and didn't even bother to look at the Crimen card before snatching the glass of orange juice from Halsey's hand. He downed the whole thing in one breath, then slammed the glass on the table. "Are you seriously gonna stand there and tell me that everything we need to know about the *real* monster we've spent all this time looking for is in a fucking *board game*?"

Owen raised a finger. "Not a board game, dude—"

"I don't give a shit!"

Halsey calmly watched her mission partner and best friend until his heavy breathing settled down and his furious scowl softened. Then she nodded and shot him a wide grin. "Looks like it."

The apartment filled with the A-Team's laughter, surprise, disbelief, and excitement to finally have found something useful. Everyone got up from their seats, abandoning the Ambrosius records, and swarmed toward the table to get a good look at the image on Owen's playing card.

Brigham blinked numbly at his best friend, oblivious to the chaotic enthusiasm all around him, then laughed. "Well, shit. Then I guess it's time to let everyone know we found our monster."

Halsey winked at him and pulled her phone from her pocket. "Time to get to work."

Get sneak peeks, exclusive giveaways, behind the scenes content, and more. PLUS you'll be notified of special **one day only fan pricing** on new releases.

Sign up today to get free stories.

Visit: https://marthacarr.com/read-free-stories/

AUTHOR NOTES - MARTHA CARR
JUNE 6, 2023

Have you been to a Pizza Friday celebration yet? Okay, some of you, maybe a lot of you, are asking, "What's a Pizza Friday?" Remember the year 2020? The one that's burned into our brains when we were all sitting at home around the world. When it started, I thought, two weeks is a long time. Maybe I can help us all to stay connected.

On one of my daily very long walks I thought, why not gather on Zoom at lunchtime and send pizzas to some people in the US (because how would I order and deliver pizza anywhere else – yes, I've been asked why it's only the US), and we can chat about books, our pets, new jobs, the weather. Whatever was on our minds.

Pizza Friday was born – and back then was every Friday at 1 pm CT. Fans gathered from everywhere around the world and we shared what we could see outside our windows, and what we had been reading.

It was supposed to be temporary. Whatever. Quarantine was supposed to be two weeks. We adjust, we make new plans. Hey, I'm an indie author. Adjust, create, move on is one of my mottos.

That was March 2020 and here we are in June 2023. Three years of pizza and gathering! Now it's once a month on the first Friday of every month and five people in the US are still winning pizzas. Sometimes someone forgets they entered and turns a pizza away. That's always fun.

There is usually about twenty people, give or take and a couple of authors stop by regularly. TR Cameron has been there every month faithfully but it wasn't till a few months ago that the regulars realized TR Cameron wasn't a pen name of mine – he was someone in their midst. We've referred to him as the AI, TR Cameron, ever since. He seems to enjoy it.

Scott Walker is another regular and they get to announce new books coming out and meet new readers.

But something else has happened over those three years. These people from different parts of the globe have become a kind of family for each other. They check on each other in between meetings and celebrate new jobs or opening a business or going into remission. And they listen when someone has lost a parent or a job or a beloved pet. There's a little bit of everything.

We've even tried to do April Fools jokes, and one month we all wore hats inspired by Demi who has an impressive and unique hat collection. Show up next month and you'll see what I mean. John looked so good in his fedora he's been wearing it to meetings ever since.

The meetings are open to anyone and everyone and the links to the entry form for the pizza and the Zoom link for the meeting are posted on my social media and in my newsletter. Plus, you get to ask me questions about my books or tell me what you liked, and we share books we love by all kinds of authors – indie and traditional, and they tend to hear about what's coming next before anyone else. Next on is on July 7th at 1 pm CT. Hope I see you there. More adventures to follow.

AUTHOR NOTES - MICHAEL ANDERLE

JUNE 5, 2023

First, thank you for not only reading this story but these author notes in the back as well!

Now that I know what I want can happen...

Apple has just announced their AR/VR goggles, and I'm salivating. Why, you ask? Well, they have everything I've been craving in such a product for years.

I'm not a newcomer to the world of AR/VR. I've owned both the Quest 01 and the Quest 02, but they never fully satisfied me. Don't get me wrong. They're fantastic pieces of technology, but they just didn't hit the right spot for me. You see, I'm not a gamer. My tech use is skewed toward business or reading.

This is where the Apple AR/VR goggles come in.

Imagine, if you will, slipping on a pair of goggles and suddenly having access to three virtual screens, each equivalent to a 32" display (plus a TV if you want it), while still being aware of your actual surroundings. The convenience, the versatility, and the potential—it is a tantalizing prospect.

I have waited for so long.

The flip side to this high-tech utopia? The price tag. At $3,499 (according to Apple this morning), this dream comes at a hefty cost. It looks like I'll have to work out the logistics of kidney-selling between now and the product release in early 2024. Of course, I'm jesting...mostly. Actually, probably not. If my wife wants one too, she's going to have to supply her own kidney.

Just saying.

The advent of these goggles reinforces a belief that I've held for a long time: technology holds limitless potential for storytelling, communication, and engagement. So, who knows? Maybe my next series will be written with the help of an array of virtual screens, SIRI dictation (that actually works), and I'm (virtually) sitting on the beach, drinking a Coke©.

Until the next book and the next set of author notes, take care!

Ad Aeternitatem,

Michael Anderle

MORE STORIES with Michael newsletter HERE: https://michael.beehiiv.com/

BOOKS BY MARTHA CARR

THE LEIRA CHRONICLES
CASE FILES OF AN URBAN WITCH
DIARY OF A DARK MONSTER
THE EVERMORES CHRONICLES
SOUL STONE MAGE
THE KACY CHRONICLES
MIDWEST MAGIC CHRONICLES
THE FAIRHAVEN CHRONICLES
I FEAR NO EVIL
THE DANIEL CODEX SERIES
SCHOOL OF NECESSARY MAGIC
SCHOOL OF NECESSARY MAGIC: RAINE CAMPBELL
ALISON BROWNSTONE
FEDERAL AGENTS OF MAGIC
SCIONS OF MAGIC
THE UNBELIEVABLE MR. BROWNSTONE
DWARF BOUNTY HUNTER
ACADEMY OF NECESSARY MAGIC
MAGIC CITY CHRONICLES
ROGUE AGENTS OF MAGIC
CHRONICLES OF WINLAND UNDERWOOD
WITCH WARRIOR

OTHER BOOKS BY JUDITH BERENS

OTHER BOOKS BY MARTHA CARR

JOIN THE ORICERAN UNIVERSE FAN GROUP ON FACEBOOK!

BOOKS BY MICHAEL ANDERLE

Sign up for the LMBPN email list to be notified of new releases and special deals!

http://lmbpn.com/email/

For a complete list of books by Michael Anderle, please visit:

www.lmbpn.com/ma-books/

CONNECT WITH THE AUTHORS

Martha Carr Social
Website:
http://www.marthacarr.com
Facebook:
https://www.facebook.com/groups/MarthaCarrFans/

Michael Anderle

Website: http://lmbpn.com

Email List: https://michael.beehiiv.com/

https://www.facebook.com/LMBPNPublishing

https://twitter.com/MichaelAnderle

https://www.instagram.com/lmbpn_publishing/

https://www.bookbub.com/authors/michael-anderle

www.ingramcontent.com/pod-product-compliance
Lightning Source LLC
LaVergne TN
LVHW091718070526
838199LV00050B/2451